Anna Ella Carroll

Miss Carroll's Claim Before Congress

asking compensation for military and other services in connection with the

Civil War

Anna Ella Carroll

Miss Carroll's Claim Before Congress
asking compensation for military and other services in connection with the Civil War

ISBN/EAN: 9783337409494

Printed in Europe, USA, Canada, Australia, Japan

Cover: Foto ©Andreas Hilbeck / pixelio.de

More available books at **www.hansebooks.com**

MISS CARROLL'S
CLAIM BEFORE CONGRESS

ASKING

COMPENSATION FOR MILITARY AND OTHER SERVICES IN CONNECTION WITH THE CIVIL WAR.

To the Honorable the Senate and House of Representatives of the United States in Congress assembled:

The memorialist, Anna Ella Carroll, respectfully represents that, as stated in her memorial heretofore submitted to Congress, she rendered important and valuable military services in the civil war, and especially that she devised the Tennessee campaign of 1862.

At the time she suggested this change of campaign, the military topography of the revolted States was very imperfectly understood, and it was therefore not surprising that the military operations for the suppression of the rebellion had not met the expectations of the country. The tide of battle thus far had been steadily against the Union. The enemy was arrayed in strong force on the Potomac, and on a line extending from thence westward through Bowling Green to Columbus, on the Mississippi. To him *time* was power, and every day's delay a continuous victory, while it increased the difficulties which were gathering and closing around the National cause.

More than seven months had been consumed since the war commenced, and it had already aggregated a debt of some $500,000,000. An army numbering between seven and eight hundred thousand men had taken the field and

$2,000,000 scarcely sufficed for its daily expenditure, beside every day was a sacrifice of hundreds of lives.

The North had become restive, and the credit of the Government was virtually exhausted. At the same time England and France were preparing and anxious to terminate the conflict by intervening, and making good the independence of the South.

Unless their unquestioned military advantage could be gained in the next few months that would satisfy the country and convince Europe of the ability of the Government to conquer the rebellion, all hope of restoring the Union was gone. How could this military advantage over the rebellion be gained in time, was then the momentous question which pressed upon every loyal heart connected with the Government.

The Army of the Potomac, on which the country had relied for success, could not, in the opinion of its commander, safely advance until the Army of the West had engaged the enemy in that quarter, and the Secretary of War, with the Adjutant General, after a tour of inspection in Octobe 1861, reported that in the judgment of the commanders the forces in Kentucky and Missouri were not strong enough to make an advance. The President was painfully apprehensive that this decisive advantage could not be gained in time.

In this crisis your memorialist perceived and pointed out to the Government how this success *could* be obtained in time.

Being convinced after careful inquiry that the Mississippi expedition, howsoever strong, could not open that river upon its waters, except at a cost, perhaps, of years and a corresponding sacrifice of life and treasure, she turned her attention to other lines of invasion and found the Tennessee river afforded sufficient depth of water for the gunboats to the Muscle Shoals in Alabama, but a few miles from the Memphis and Charleston railroad—the enemy's only complete interior line of communication—your memorialist

comprehended that the movement of a strong force up
that river to a position in command of *that* railroad, would
effectually cut the confederacy in two by severing the Atlantic from the Missippi portion—turn Columbus and all the
the fortifications on the Mississippi to Memphis—free all
Western Kentucky and Tennessee from the enemy, and bring
the whole of that country southward to Mobile under the control of the national arms. And she indicated as the position, Hamburg on the west bank of the Tennessee river,
which, it will be observed, is but two or three miles from
Pittsburg Landing. These suggestions she embodied in
the following paper and submitted it to the Government the
30th of November, 1861 :

The civil and military authorities seem to be laboring
under a great mistake in regard to the true key of the war
in the Southwest. *It is not the Mississippi but the Tennessee
river.* All the military preparations made in the West indi-
cate that the Mississippi river is the point to which the
authorities are directing their attention. On that river many
battles must be fought and heavy risks incurred before any
impression can be made on the enemy, all of which could
be avoided by using the Tennessee river. This river is navigable for middle class boats to the foot of the Muscle Shoals
in Alabama, and is open to navigation all the year, while
the distance is but two hundred and fifty miles by the river
from Paducah, on the Ohio. The Tennessee offers many
advantages over the Mississippi. We should avoid the
almost impregnable batteries of the enemy, which cannot
be taken without great danger and great risk of life to our
forces, from the fact that our boats, if crippled, would fall a
prey to the enemy by being swept by the current to him,
and away from the relief of our friends. But even should
we succeed, still we will only have begun the war, for we
shall then have to fight the country from whence the enemy
derives his supplies.

Now, an advance up the Tennessee river would avoid
this danger; for, *if our boats were crippled, they would drop
back with the current and escape capture.*

But a still greater advantage would be its tendency *to cut
the enemy's lines in two, by reaching the Memphis and Charleston
railroad,* threatening Memphis, which lies one hundred
miles due west, and no defensible point between; also

Nashville, only ninety miles northeast, and Florence and Tuscumbia, in North Alabama, forty miles east. A movement in this direction would do more to relieve our friends in Kentucky, and inspire the loyal hearts in East Tennessee than the possession of the whole of the mississippi river. If well executed, *it would cause the evacuation of all the formidable fortifications* upon which the rebels ground their hopes for success; and, in the event of our fleet attacking Mobile, the presence of our troops in the northern part of Alabama *would be material aid to the fleet.*

Again, the aid our forces would receive from the loyal men in Tennessee would enable them soon to crush the last traitor in that region, and *the separation of the two extremes* would do more than one hundred battles for the Union cause.

The Tennessee river is crossed by the Memphis and Louisville railroad and the Memphis and Nashville railroad. At Hamburg the river makes the big bend on the east, touching the northeast corner of Mississippi, entering the northwest corner of Alabama, forming an arc to the south, entering the State of Tennessee at the northeast corner of Alabama, and if it does not touch the northwest corner of Georgia, comes very near it. It is but eight miles from Hamburg to Memphis and Charleston railroad, which goes through Tuscumbia, only two miles from the river, which it crosses at Decatur, thirty miles above, intersecting with the Nashville and Chattanooga road at Stephenson. The Tennessee river has never less than three feet to Hamburg on the "shoalest" bar, and, during the fall, winter, and spring months, there is always water for the largest boats that are used on the Mississippi river. It follows from the above facts that in making the Mississippi the key to the war in the West, or rather in overlooking the Tennessee river, the subject is not understood by the superiors in command.

On the 5th of January, 1862, she communicated some additional facts, of which the following is an extract:

Having given you my views of the Tennessee river on my return from the West, showing that this river *is the true strategical key to overcome the rebels in the southwest,* I beg again to recur to the importance of its adoption. This river is never impeded by ice in the coldest winter, as the Mississippi and Cumberland sometimes are. I ascertained, when in St. Louis, that the gunboats then fitting out could not retreat against the current of the western rivers, and so stated to you; beside, their principal guns are placed forward, and will not be very efficient against an enemy below them. The fighting would have to be done by their stern guns, only two, or if they anchored by the stern, they would lose the advantage of motion, which would prevent the enemy from getting their range. Our gunboats, at anchor, would be a target which the enemy will not be slow to improve and benefit thereby.

The Tennessee river, beginning at Paducah, fifty miles above Cairo, after leaving the Ohio, runs across south-southeast, rather than through Kentucky and Tennessee, until it reaches the Mississippi line, directly west of Florence and Tuscumbia, which lie fifty miles east, and Memphis, one hundred and twenty-five miles west, with the Memphis and Charleston railroad eight miles from the river. There is no difficulty in reaching this point any time of the year, and the water is known to be deeper than on the Ohio.

If you will look on the map of the Western States you will see in what a position Buckner would be placed by a strong advance up the Tennessee river. He would be obliged to back out of Kentucky, or if he did not our forces could take Nashville in his rear, and compel him to lay down his arms.

The Government comprehended the transcendent importance of her suggestions, accepted them, inaugurated the campaign upon them, and the decisive blow was struck, which cut the Confederate power in two, coerced the evacuation of all the formidable fortifications on the Mississippi from Columbus to Memphis; averted European intervention and consequent war with the United States removed the visible and growing discontent in the great Northwest; revived the National credit, and hurled the enemy back to the Vicksburg and Meridian railroad, and brought the national forces in contact with the slave population of the cotton States, which turned four millions of people, until then a source of his strength against him, and to the support of the Union.

That the danger from financial bankruptcy and European intervention and invasion may be more fully apprehended, which in those supreme moments made the very existence of the Government a question of doubt, and to show more, clearly that the victories in the West were not achieved a day to soon *to prevent defeat and the loss of the Union,* your memorialist asks your attention to the extracts from the speeches of many distinguished statesmen of that period in both Houses of Congress, many of whom were occupying positions on the most important committees connected with the prosecution of the war, and necessarily possessed of the most accurate information. (See Appendix 1.)

So soon as the victories revealed that the Government was in very fact advancing the army on a *definite* plan to the destruction of the rebellion, the enthusiasm of the people and of Congress was thoroughly aroused, and not knowing who had projected the campaign in the exultation of the hour, they ascribed the honor to one and another as their partiality or favoritism inclined. In this connection your memorialist respectfully invites your attention to the discussion upon the resolution of Mr. Roscoe Conkling in the House of Representatives, on the 24th of February, 1862, the object of which was to ascertain " *whether these victories were organized or directed at a distance from the fields where they were won, and if so, by whom organized, or whether they were the conceptions of those who executed them.*"

She also invites your attention to the subsequent remarks of Mr. Washburn, in the House, and Mr. Grimes, Chairman of the Naval Committee, in the Senate. (See Appendix 2.)

With the knowledge that the Government was acting upon the information communicated by her, your memorialist contributed other suggestions as the campaign progressed.

Immediately after the fall of Fort Henry she suggested to the Secretary of War the practicability of advancing the army onward to Mobile or Vicksburg. Her duplicate of this letter she has not as yet been able to find, but it may be observed there is an allusion to it in her letter of October, 1862, on the reduction of Vicksburg.

In view of the disappointment manifested at the check

which the naval flotilla received at Island 10, and with perfect confidence that the campaign would accomplish every result, as promised by the suggestions in November, your memorialist addressed the Secretary of War the 26th of March, 1862, of which the following is an extract:

The failure to take Island 10, which thus far occasions much disappointment to the country, excites no surprise to me. When I looked at the gunboats at St. Louis, and was informed as to their power, and considered that the current of the Mississippi at full tide runs at the rate of five miles per hour, which is very near the speed of our gunboats, I could not resist the conclusion that they were not well fitted to the taking of batteries on the Mississippi river if assisted by gunboats perhaps equal to our own. Hence it was that I wrote Col. Scott from there that the Tennessee river was our strategic point, and the successes at Forts Henry and Donelson established the justice of those observations. *Had our victorious army, after the fall of Fort Henry, immediately pushed up the Tennessee river and taken position on the Memphis and Charleston railroad, between Corinth, Mississippi, and De-catur, Alabama, which might easily have been done at that time with a small force, every rebel soldier in Western Kentucky and Tennessee would have fled from every position to the south of that railroad.* And had Buell pursued the enemy in his retreat from Nashville without delay into a commanding position in North Alabama on the railroad between Chattanooga and Decatur, the rebel government at Richmond would have necessarily been obliged to retreat to the cotton States. I am fully satisfied that the true policy of Gen. H. is to strengthen Grant's column by such a force as will enable him *at once to seize the Memphis and Charleston railroad, as it is the readiest means of reducing Island 10, and all the strongholds of the enemy to Memphis.*

And again observing in October, 1862, preparations for a naval attack on Vicksburg she wrote as follows:

As I understand an expedition is about to go down the river for the purpose of reducing Vicksburg, I have prepared the enclosed map in order to demonstrate more clearly the obstacles to be encountered in the contemplated assault. In the first place *it is impossible to take Vicksburg in front without too great a loss of life and material*, for the reason that the river is only about half a mile wide, and our forces would be in point-blank range of their guns—not only from their water-batteries which line the shore, but from the batteries that crown the hills, while the enemy would be protected by the elevation from the range of our fire. By examining the map I enclose, you will at once perceive why a place of so little apparent strength has been enabled to resist the combined fleets of the Upper and Lower Mississippi. *The most economical plan for the reduction of Vicksburg now, is to push a column from Memphis or Corinth down the Mississippi Central railroad to Jackson, the capital of* the State of Mississippi. The *occupation of Jackson and the command of the railroad to New Orleans would compel the immediate evacuation of Vicksburg* as well as the retreat of the entire rebel army east of that line; and by another movement of our army from Jackson, Mississippi, or from Corinth to Meredian in the State of Mississippi, on the Ohio and Mobile railroad, especially if aided by a movement of our gunboats on Mobile, the confederate forces, with all the disloyal men and their slaves would be compelled to fly east of the Tombigbee.

Mobile being then in our possession with 100,000 men at Meridian would redeem the entire country from Memphis to the Tombigbee river. Of course, I would have the gunboats with a small force at Vicksburg as auxiliary to this movement. With regard to the canal, Vicksburg can be rendered useless to the confederate army upon the very first rise of the river, but I do not advise this, because Vicksburg belongs to the United States, and we desire to hold and fortify it, for the Mississippi river at Vicksburg and the Vicksburg and Jackson railroad will become necessary as a base of our future operations. *Vicksburg might have been reduced eight months ago, as I then advised after the fall of Fort Henry, and with much more ease than it can be done to-day.*

Other papers upon military operations were contributed by your memorialist during the progress of the war, but those only are given which relate to the Tennessee campaign.

Your memorialist now respectfully submits that a comparison of these papers with the official history of the military operations in that quarter will show that the plan of these campaigns is distinctly and clearly set forth in her paper of November 30, 1861, and the subsequent letters in relation thereto. The correctness of this plan was proven not alone by the successes which awaited upon its execution, but likewise by the failures to open the Mississippi or win any decided success on the plan first devised by the Government.

That the advantages gained by the campaign were not pressed to the final conquest of the rebellion in '62, '63, does not in the least impair the value of the plan, since the merit is in the *conception* rather than its execution. For when the Government was shown the decisive position in the geographical centre of the rebel power, with a navigable river for a line of communication with the North, which the enemy could neither break nor destroy, the *mastery* of the rebellion by the National arms was ever more assured, even though the powers of all Europe should be arrayed upon its side. This campaign having therefore decided the issues of our great war, must ever rank with those very few strategic movements in the world's history which have settled the fate of empires and nations. Hence a more extended account of its origin and development might seem to be demanded than that which has heretofore been presented.

Your memorialist, under an agreement with the War Department to write in aid of the Union, and with the hope of rendering greater efficiency, visited the West in the autumn of '61 for the purpose of studying the condition of affairs in that military department. Soon after she arrived her attention was arrested by the confidence with which the best informed Southern sympathisers in that section expressed the opinion that the Government could not suppress the rebellion ; that the Army of the Potomac, no matter how strong it might be made, could not reach Richmond before summer, and that Columbus would effectually bar any advance down the Mississippi ; that before spring Price would redeem the whole of Missouri, and Buckner the whole of Kentucky, and the Confederate flag would be planted on the Northern border of the slave States, when it would become the material interest of the Northwest to stop the war and compel the government to come to terms with the South. These declarations were having a most depressing effect upon the loyal sentiment in that section. Your memorialist realizing the imminency of the danger that environed the Union, directed her inquiries as to the best means of escape. Her anxiety in regard to the success of the Mississippi expedition was increased by the opinion expressed by Judge Evans, of Texas, who, from personal observation, was accurately acquainted with the topography of the Mississippi valley, whose attention had been called to this plan of campaign by Secretary Chase when in Washington some time before, who wished his opinion upon the proposed movement, and in view of the difficulties, Mr. Chase expressed his own doubts and his preference for an overland expedition through Cumberland Gap, Chatanooga, Atlanta, and thence to the sea.

Your memorialist then resolved to seek the information of practical steamboat men as to their views of the Mississippi expedition. She met in the hotel at St. Louis Mrs. Scott, whose husband, Captain C. M. Scott, a pilot, was connected with the expedition, and requested to see him, and on his return to St. Louis after the battle of Belmont she sent for him. Her energies were quickened at this time by the sight of the battle-torn regiment, the Seventh Iowa, as it filed into Benton Barracks. She learned from Captain Scott, who was a very intelligent and experienced pilot on the Mississippi, that it would be impossible to reduce Columbus with the gunboats without a very 'arge co-operating land force, and after a very long siege; that the gunboats were not suited to fight down the Mississippi, on account of its strong current; that there were a great many positions on the Mississippi that the enemy could make as strong as Columbus; that they would be fortified as our fleet descended, so that innumerable battles must be fought, and it would take years to open that river; and this, he said, was the belief of every pilot connected with the expedition. He said the Cumberland, at favorable stages of water, was navigable for the gunboats to Nashville, and the Tennessee at all stages to the Muscle Shoals, in Alabama. Upon the mention of the navigability of the Tennessee river for gunboats to the Muscle Shoals, in Alabama, the thought flashed upon the mind of your memorialist that all the fortifications on the Mississippi might be turned by advancing the army up the Tennessee river to a position in North Mississippi or Alabama. She immediately communicated this thought to Judge Evans, and asked him if it could not be done; he concurred that it could, and after reflecting a moment, said, "That's the move." Your memorialist said, "I will have it done." She invited him to join in the interview. In answer to our inquiries, Captain Scott stated the draft and speed of the gunboats and number of guns; the width and depth of the channel of the Mississippi; the number of bluffs upon the river, and the wide extent of the swamp or overflowed lands; also the width and depth of the channel of the Cumberland and Tennessee rivers. He did not think the gunboats could pass over the Muscle Shoals, in Alabama. We inquired as to the practicability of the naval expedition reaching Mobile, and as to the navigability of the Alabama and Tombigbee rivers. He thought the fleet could not pass the bar, some seven miles below that city; said the Tombigbee afforded good steamboat navigation to Demopolis, which is one hundred and fifty miles from the Muscle Shoals, in the Tennessee river.

Your memorialist requested this gentleman to give her a memorandum of the facts elicited and informed him that it was her purpose to induce the Government, if possible, to change the plan upon which they were operating and divert the expedition up the Tennessee river, and in the event of the change, requested him to furnish her with all the facts he could obtain during his continuance with the expedition.

She hastened to Washington and prepared her paper upon the data she collected, and laid it before the Government the 30th of November, 1861, as hereinbefore stated.

Col. Scott, to whom she read it in the War Department, had then control of the railroads used by the Government, and was accurately informed upon the railroad system of the South and its value in war. He saw at once that the seizure of Memphis and Charleston railroad at *that point* would not only open the Mississippi, but would open the way for McClellan's march on Richmond. He expressed great gratification and said it was the first solution of the difficulty, and he had no doubt but your memorialist was *right.* He asked her for the paper; she told him it was for the use of the Government she had prepared it, and said to him, repeating the language, " if it is upon the expedition to descend the Mississippi that you rely to save the Union, then there is an end of it, but if you will have that expedition diverted up the Tennessee river, you will not only save the Union, but cover yourself with glory."

As these suggestions did not come from any one connected with the military or naval service, it was deemed prudent that the Government should appropriate them without any reference to their source.

She left the paper without signature, caring absolutely nothing in those supreme moments, if it but saved the country, whether it should be denied or forgotten that she was its author.

Convinced of the importance of her suggestions, Colonel Scott requested your memorialist to continue her labors, and contribute all she deemed important during the war. He submitted the paper to the Secretary of War and President Lincoln. The President had from the beginning reserved special direction of the Mississippi expedition, now, decided the Tennessee river as the line of invasion. And when Secretary Stanton came into the Department, the middle of January, 1862, the campaign was inaugurated, and Colonel Scott, under the instructions of the Government, went forward to arrange to increase the effective force of the Western armies as rapidly as possible for the purpose of carrying it through.

In proof that your memorialist submitted the plan of campaign, as set forth in her memorial, and that the government profited thereby, she offers the following from Hon. Thomas A. Scott, Assistant Secretary of War:

PHILADELPHIA, *June* 15, 1870.

I learn from Miss Carroll that she has a claim before Congress for services rendered in the year 1861, in aid of the Government. I believe the Government ought now to reward her liberally for the efforts she made in its behalf. I hope you will be able to pass some measure that will give Miss Carroll *what she is most certainly entitled to.*

THOMAS A. SCOTT.

Hon. JACOB M. HOWARD,
    United States Senate.

PHILADELPHIA, *June* 24, 1870.

On or about the 30th of November, 1861, Miss Carroll, as stated in her memorial, called on me, as Assistant Secretary of War, and *suggested the propriety of abandoning the expedition which was then preparing to descend the Mississippi river and to adopt instead the Tennessee river, and handed to me the plan of campaign, as appended to her memorial,* which plan I submitted to the Secretary of War, and its general ideas were adopted. On my return from the Southwest, in 1862, I informed Miss Carroll, as she states in her memorial, that through the adoption of this plan the country had been saved millions, and that it entitled her to the kind consideration of Congress.

THOMAS A. SCOTT.

Hon. JACOB M. HOWARD,
    Of the *Military Committee of the United States Senate.*

Again :

PHILADELPHIA, *May* 1, 1872.

MY DEAR SIR: I take pleasure in stating that the plan presented by Miss Carroll, in November, 1861, for a campaign upon the Tennessee river and thence South, was submitted to the Secretary of War and President Lincoln. And, after Secretary Stanton's appointment, I was directed to go to the Western armies and arrange to increase their effective force as rapidly as possible. A part of the duty assigned me was the organization and consolidation into regiments of all the troops then being recruited in Ohio, Indiana, Illinois, and Michigan, for the purpose of carrying through *this campaign, then inaugurated.*

This work was vigorously prosecuted by the army, and, as the valuable suggestions of Miss Carroll, made to the Department some months before, *were substantially carried out through the campaigns in that section*—great successes followed, and the country was largely benefitted in the saving of time and expenditure.

I hope Congress will reward Miss Carroll liberally for her patriotic efforts and services.

Very truly, yours,   THOMAS A. SCOTT.

Hon. HENRY WILSON,

Chairman Military Committee, U. S. Senate.

That President Lincoln and Secretary Stanton fully recognized the service of your memorialist will appear from the following letter of the Hon. B. F. Wade, Chairman of the "Committee on the Conduct of the War:"

WASHINGTON, *February* 28, 1872.

To the Chairman of the Military Committee of the United States Senate :

DEAR SIR: I have been requested to make a brief statement of what I can recollect concerning the claim of Miss Carroll, now before Congress. From my position as chairman of the Committee on the Conduct of the War, it came to my knowledge that the expedition which was preparing, under the special direction of President Lincoln, to descend the Mississippi river, was abandoned, and the Tennessee expedition was adopted by the Government in pursuance of information and a plan presented to the Secretary of War, I think in the latter part of November, 1861, by Miss Carroll. A copy of this plan was put in my hands immediately after the fall of Forts Henry and Donelson. With the knowledge of its author, I interrogated witnesses before the committee to ascertain how far military men were cognizant of the fact. Subsequently, *President Lincoln informed me that the merit of this plan was due to Miss Carroll; that the transfer of the armies from Cairo and the northern part of Kentucky to the Memphis and Charleston railroad was her conception, and was afterwards carried out generally, and very much in detail, according to her suggestions. Secretary Stanton also conversed with me on the matter, and fully recognized Miss Carroll's service to the Union in the organization of this campaign.* Indeed, both Mr. Lincoln and Mr. Stanton, the latter only a few weeks before his death, expressed to me their high appreciation *of this service,* and all the other services she was enabled to render the country by her influence and ability as a writer, and they both expressed the wish that the Government would reward her liberally for the same, in which I most fully concur.

B. F. WADE.

As more conclusively showing the appreciation in which Secretary Stanton held the services of your memorialist, she submits the following correspondence with Judge Wade:

MARCH 28, 1873.

MY DEAR JUDGE WADE: I took a memorandum at the time of some remarks of yours to me in a conversation we had in January, 1870. Alluding to the recent death of Secretary Stanton, you said I "had lost a strong friend in him," and repeated several remarks he made to you respecting myself in connection with the services I had rendered the country in the civil war. I inquired how long since this was said? You replied, "why the very last time I ever saw him; only a few weeks before he died. I was with him on that occasion four hours. He voluntarily spoke of you, and said there was one person who had done more to save this country than all the rest of the border State people together, and who to that time had had no proper recognition or reward for it." I asked him who he meant? He said, "Why, Miss Carroll." I told him I had always known that. He said, "*if his life was spared, he intended you should be properly recognized and rewarded for originating the Tennessee campaign, that the merit belonged to you, and he would see you through Congress if he lived.*" Your remarks, coming so recently from Mr. Stanton, impressed me very much, especially as they accorded so fully with what he said himself to me some two years before. I would be pleased if you can recall what I have stated.

With great esteem,

S. E. CARROLL.

WASHINGTON, *March* 31, 1873.

MISS CARROLL: I have received your note in which you desire me to state the language in which Mr. Stanton expressed himself in reference to your services during and after the war, the substance of which you already have. I remember that he stated those sentiments with great earnestness, but after such a length of time I cannot undertake to state the exact language that he used, but when I related to you what he said, so soon after the event, I doubt not that I used or rather *repeated* very nearly the language he used in expressing himself to me, and there is nothing in your relation of what I told you, that conflicts with my recollection of his language to me.

Yours truly,

B. F. WADE.

Hon. O. H. Browning, of Illinois, Senator during the war, and in confidential relations with President Lincoln and Secretary Stanton, refers in the following letter to the estimation in which they held military services of your memorialist:

QUINCY, ILLNOIS, *Sept.* 17*th*, 1873.

MISS A. E. CARROLL: During the progress of the war of the rebellion, from 1861 to 1865, I had frequent conversations with President Lincoln and Secretary Stanton in regard to the active and efficient part you had taken in behalf of the country, in all of which they expressed their admiration of and gratitude for the patriotic and valuable services you had rendered the cause of the Union—and the hope that you would be adequately compensated by Congress. At this late day I cannot recall the details of those conversations, but am sure that the salutatory influence of *your publications upon public opinion* and *your suggestions in connection with the important military movements were among the meritorius services which they recognized as entitled to remuneration.*

In addition to the large debt of gratitude which the country owes you, I am sure you are entitled to generous pecuniary compensation, which I trust will not be withheld. With sentiments of high regard,

I am your obedient servant,

O. H. BROWNING.

In confirmation of her own statement as to the conception and development of the plan of the Tennessee campaign, your memorialist submits the statement made by Chief Justice Evans, of the Supreme Court of Texas, to the Chairman of the Senate Military Committee of the 42d Congress:

WASHINGTON, *April* 27, 1872.

SIR: Having been requested to state my knowledge of the Tennessee plan of campaign, I respectfully submit that Miss Carroll was the first to suggest to the Government the practicability and importance of moving the armies from Cairo up the Tennessee river into Northern Mississippi or Alabama, on the Memphis and Charleston railroad.

It may be remembered that the rebel power very early in the contest developed a strength and proportion which the country was not prepared to expect. This fact, together with our failure to achieve any early military success, was having a most depressing effect upon the spirit of the country, while the danger of foreign intervention was becoming more and more imminent. Indeed, our Government was warned that without some decided military advantage before spring, England and France would acknowledge the independence of the South, and raise the blockade for a supply of cotton. If, then, we would preserve the Union, we must in a very short period gain a strategic position South that would satisfy the country, and convince European powers of the ability of the Government to suppress the rebellion.

To find this decisive point, and the direction in which a blow could be delivered that would insure this result, became in the autumn of 1861 a matter of the most serious military consideration. It was in this exigency that Miss Carroll visited the West in quest of information in aid of the Union, as she stated to me, and as I fully believe.

From early in October to about the 20th of November, 1861, she was at the Everett House, in Saint Louis. I was also in that city, and conversed almost every day with her upon the military and political situation in that quarter, and especially in reference to the difficulties to be overcome by the expedition preparing to open the Mississippi· I am, therefore, able from personal knowledge to state the origin of the plan of the Tennessee campaign from its inception to its final draught and presentation to the War Department. The conception which is embodied in this plan occurred to the mind of Miss Carroll about the middle of November, 1861, in conversation with Mr. Charles M. Scott, a pilot on one of the transports connected with the expedition to descend the Mississippi river. She learned some important facts from his wife, whom she met in the hotel, concerning the naval preparations for the expedition, and requested to see her husband that she might be informed as to the special knowledge and opinions of practical steamboatmen, and on his arrival in Saint Louis, after the battle of Belmont, she sent for him.

When he stated to her that it was his opinion, and that of the pilots generally who were familiar with the western waters, that the naval expedition could not open the Mississippi; that the Gunboats were not fitted to fight down that river, and that it was practicable for them to go up the Tennessee, the thought occurred to her that the Government should direct the Mississippi expedition up the Tennessee river to some point in Northern Mississippi or Alabama, so as to command the Memphis and Charleston railroad. In a very earnest and animated manner she communicated this thought to me. Being a native of that section, and intimately acquainted with its geography, and particularly with the Tennessee river, I was at once impressed with the tremendous value of her suggestions. She immediately introduced Captain Scott to me with a request that I would interrogate him on all his special facts. He stated the number and strength of the fortifications on the Mississippi and the impossibility of the gunboats to reduce them, the width and depth of the Tennessee river, and the practicability of ascending with the gunboats to the foot of the Muscle Shoals, but did not think they could pass above.

With the view of ascertaining the practicability of a naval expedition to reach Mobile and ascend the Alabama and Tombigbee rivers, I questioned him as to the depth of these waters also. We were so impressed with the fullness and accuracy of his information, that Miss Carroll asked him to write it down for her, to do which he declined, as he said, from want of education, but finally consented. The same day she wrote from St. Louis to Attorney General Bates, and Hon. Thomas A. Scott, Assistant Secretary of War, suggesting the exchange of the expedition from the Mississippi to the Tennessee river, and on her arrival in Washington, the latter part of November, she prepared the plan of campaign appended to her memorial, and submitted it to me for my opinion, and, without signature, placed the same in the hands of Thomas A. Scott to be used by the Government without her name being known in its connection.

She communicated with the pilot, Captain Scott, at Cairo, what she had done, and the probabilities that her suggestions would be adopted by the Government, and requested him to send her from time to time all the information he could gather. He complied with her request, and gave her further important information, from which she prepared a second paper on the Tennessee campaign of January 5, 1862, an imperfect copy of which appears in Mr. Howard's report. I say imperfect, because I have a very distinct recollection of aiding her in the preparation of that paper, tracing with her, upon a map of the United States which hung in her parlor, the Memphis and Charleston railroad and its connections southward, the course of the Tennessee, the Alabama, and Tombigbee rivers, and the position of Mobile Bay; and when Henry fell, she wrote the Department showing the feasibility of going either to Mobile or Vicksburg.

In conclusion, I will state that having critically examined

all the plans of our generals and everything official which has been published by the War Department bearing on this point, and every history that has been written upon the war, it is evident that, up to the time Miss Carroll submitted her plan to the Government, it had not occurred to any military mind that the *true line of invasion was not down the Mississippi river, nor yet up the Cumberland to Nashville, and thence overland, but that it was the Tennessee river, and on that line alone, that the Mississippi could be opened and the power of the rebellion destroyed.*

It had not been perceived that moving a force up the Tennessee river into Northern Mississippi or Alabama strong enough to maintain itself and command the Memphis and Charleston railroad would render all the fortifications from Bowling Green to Columbus and from Columbus to Memphis *valueless* to the enemy, and cause their evacuation and bring the whole Mississippi Valley under the control of the national arms.

Respectfully submitted.

L. D. EVANS.

Hon. HENRY WILSON,
Chairman of the Military Committee of the U. S. Senate.

Your memorialist's connection with this campaign was for military reasons, known only to a few friends outside of the War Department, to whom she confidentially exhibited her paper at the time, among these was Judge Whittlesey, of Ohio, who, after the fall of Henry and Donelson, asked for a copy of her plan for the purpose of endorsing his appreciation of the service, and bequeathing it as a legacy to his children. She was permitted, by his son in Mansfield, Ohio, to see this paper for the first time in December last, of which the following is a copy:

TREASURY DEPARTMENT, COMPTROLLER'S OFFICE,
February 20, 1862.

This will accompany copies of two letters written by Miss Anna Ella Carroll to the War Department. Having informed me of the contents of the letters, I requested her to permit me to copy her duplicates. When she brought them to me, she enjoined prudence in their use. They are very extraordinary papers as verified by the result. So far as I know or believe, our unparalleled victories on the Tennessee and Cumberland rivers may be traced to her sagacious observations and intelligence. Her views were as broad and sagacious as the field to be occupied. In selecting the Tennessee and Cumberland rivers instead of the Mississippi, she set at naught the opinions of civilians, of military and naval men. Justice should be done her patriotic discernment. She labors for her country and for her whole country.

ELISHA WHITTLESEY.

Your memorialist invites your attention to the following letters received from distinguished men who have examined her claim:

BALTIMORE, *October* 12, 1872.

MY DEAR MISS CARROLL: I have examined as far as I have been able, because of pressing engagements, the papers you placed in my hands relating to your claim for services rendered the Government during the civil war. That very valuable services were rendered, and that they contributed very materially to the success of the Union arms in the West is very satisfactorily established. Amongst other proofs, the letters of Messrs. Wade and Scott are conclusive. Each had the best means of knowing what your services were and how valuable they proved in their result. Every fair-minded man, with this evidence before him, will, I am sure, concur in the opinion that you should be liberally compensated by the Government. And hoping this may be so, I remain, with regard, your friend and obedient servant,

REVERDY JOHNSON.

Hon. George Vickers, United States Senator, writes:

CHESTERTOWN, MD., *July* 19, 1872.

* * * I have read a printed copy of your memorial and exhibits with a great deal of pleasure, and concluded your case was a much stronger one than I had been apprised of. The letters of Judge Evans, Mr. Wade, and Mr. Scott are explicit, pointed, and strong. There can be no doubt that you originated the plan of the Tennessee campaign, and of its subsequent adoption by the Administration.

Very sincerely, yours,
GEORGE VICKERS.

Hon. Truman Smith, of Connecticut, 20th of January, 1873, says:

I trust that whilst land, and rank, and pensions are allowed union men, that the union women who risked life and health, as well in the sanitary and in other departments, should share those similar rewards.

Be that as it may, your case stands out unique—for you towered above all our generals in military genius, and it would be a shame upon our country if you were not honored with the gratitude of all and solid pecuniary reward.

C. M. CLAY.

Again Mr. Clay refers to the claim of your memorialist.

WHITE HALL, MADISON COUNTY,
KENTUCKY, *April*, 23, 1873.

MY DEAR MISS CARROLL: Your favor enclosing your letter to Dr. Draper is received. After the exhaustive proof of your being the projector of the Tennessee line of attack upon the confederacy, it seems a waste of time to consider General Halleck's claim. * * * Were he proven capable of such a conception as Dr. Draper awards him, your presentation of the case is conclusive against its actuality.

I cannot believe that Congress will hesitate to admit your claim with all honor and substantial pecuniary reward—compensation such as all Governments bestow upon those who assist in saving their nation.

Perhaps I am all the more interested in your case because of your historic name, and because it seems to me that those of the South who stood by the Union of these States, gave higher proof of disinterested patriotism than any other citizen of the Republic.

C. M. CLAY.

The following is from Hon. J. T. Headley, the distinguished historian of the civil war:

NEWBURG, N. Y., *February* 6, 1873.

MY DEAR MADAM: I am much obliged for the pamphlet you sent me. * * * *I never knew before with whom the plan of the campaign up the Tennessee river originated.* There seemed to be a mystery attached to it that I could not solve. * * * Though General Buel sent me an immense amount of documents relating to this campaign, I could find no reference to the origin of the change of plan. Afterwards I saw it attributed to Halleck, which I knew to be false, and I noticed he never corroborated it. It is strange that, after all my research, it has rested with you to

enlighten me. *Money cannot pay for the plan of that campaign.*
I doubt not Congress   *   *   *   will show, not liberality, but some justice in the matter.

Yours, very sincerely,

J. T. HEADLEY.

The Military Committee of the United States Senate, at
the third session of the Forty-first Congress, reported (No.
339) that your memorialist did furnish the plan of the Tennessee campaign, and that it was adopted by the Government; and they further reported that, in view of her highly
meritorious services throughout the whole period of our
national troubles, and *especially at that epoch of the war to
which her memorial makes reference*, and in consideration of
the further fact that all the expenses incident to these services were borne by herself, *the committee believe her claim to
be just, and that it ought to be recognized by Congress.*

In preferring her claim for originating the Tennessee
campaign, your memorialist detracts not from the fame of
any one, for, so far as she is aware, no one has ever laid claim
to it ; and she has carefully examined every official order,
letter, and telegram hitherto published in connection with
this campaign.   And she now submits, had these papers
your memorialist laid before the Government—suggesting
the Tennessee campaign in advance of all others—been the
work of one in the military or naval service, would he not
have been heralded as the foremost strategist of the war?
Would he not have been commissioned to the highest grade
of the service and insured corresponding pay for life?   In
the name of all that is just and equal, can you withhold a
similar recognition from one on whom, in the hour of the
nation's desperate emergency, the Government relied, because not trained under the rules and axioms of war?

Other services were rendered by your memorialist.   She
wrote and published in aid of the Union from the inception
of the rebellion to its close.   In the summer of 1861 she published a reply to the speech of Senator Breckenridge, delivered in the July session of Congress.   Colonel Scott, Assist-

ant Secretary of War, to whom she was referred by the Secretary, decided to circulate a large edition as a war measure. At the same time she had an agreement to write other pamphlets in aid of the Union, and particularly upon the power of the Government in the conduct of the civil war, to be submitted to the Department for approval, and if approved, to be paid their value. Under this agreement the second, entitled the "War Powers of the Government," was submitted to the Department in December, 1861, examined, approved, and its publication ordered; but she was requested to wait for settlement until another appropriation.

The third, entitled "The Relations of the Revolted Citizens to the National Government," was written to meet the express views of President Lincoln, to whom it was directly submitted, and by him approved in advance of publication. At his request she prepared several papers on the colonization of the freedmen, a measure in which at the time he evinced great interest. And she wrote and published subsequently, on various subjects, as they were evoked by the war, and throughout the struggle, without any reference to pecuniary compensation.

For the writing, publishing, and circulation of these, prepared under the auspices of Government, your memorialist presented an account of $6,750.

Hon. Thomas A. Scott, with whom the agreement was had, having left the Department before her account was presented, wrote as follows to Hon. John Tucker, then Assistant Secretary of War:

PHILADELPHIA, *January,* 16, 1863.

HON. JOHN TUCKER, *Assistant Secretary of War:*

I believe Miss Carroll has fairly earned and ought to be paid the amount of her bill, ($6,750,) and if you will pay her I will certify to such form as you may think necessary as a voucher.

THOMAS A. SCOTT.

To Assistant Secretary Watson, who had the settlement of the claim, he wrote the following:

PHILADELPHIA, *January* 28, 1863.

All my interviews with Miss Carroll were in my official capacity as Assistant Secretary of War. The pamphlets published were, to a certain extent, under a general authority then exercised by me in the discharge of public duties as Assistant Secretary of War. No price was fixed, *but it was understood that the Government would treat her with sufficient liberality to compensate her for any service she might render.*

I thought them then, and still believe they were, of great value to the Government, and that she fairly earned and should be paid the amount she has charged, which I would have allowed in my official capacity, and which is certified as reasonable by many of the leading men of the country.

THOMAS A. SCOTT.

Assistant Secretary of War Watson subsequently paid $750 of this claim. This amount scarcely sufficed to defray the actual cost of the publications. She received nothing for the time and labor in their preparation, yet they were prepared with the understanding she whould be compensated somewhat in proportion to their value to the Government.

The creation of an intelligent and healthful public opinion at that time was as essential to the preservation of the Union as the creation and maintenance of armies in the field. As to the influence exerted upon public sentiment by these publications, your memorialist submits the following from the report of the Senate Military Committee in the 41st Congress, made through Senator Jacob M. Howard:

"From the high social position of Miss Carroll and her established ability as a writer and thinker, she was prepared at the inception of the rebellion to exercise a strong influence in behalf of Liberty and the Union. That it was felt and respected in Maryland during the darkest hours in that State's history, there can be no question. Her publications throughout the struggle were eloquently and ably written and widely circulated, and did much to arouse and invigorate the sentiment of loyalty in Maryland and other border States. *It is not too much to say that they were among the very ablest pub-*

lications of the time, and exerted a powerful influence upon the hearts of the people. Some of these publications were prepared under the auspices of the War Department, and for these Miss Carroll preferred a claim to reimburse her for the expenses incurred in their publication, *which ought to have been paid.*"

She also submits the opinions of some of the eminent men at that period:

Hon. Edward Bates, Attorney General, on the 21st of September, 1861—

I have this moment, 11 o'clock Saturday night, finished reading your most admirable reply to the speech of Mr. Breckenridge. And now, my dear lady, I have only time to thank you for taking the trouble to embody for the use of others so much sound constitutional doctrine and so many valuable historical facts in a form so compact and manageable. The President received a copy left for him and requested me to thank you cordially for your able support.

This delay was not voluntary on my part. For some time past my time and mind have been painfully engrossed by very urgent public duties, and my best affections stirred by the present condition of *Missouri*, my own neglected and almost ruined State. And this is the reason why I have been so long deprived of the pleasure and instruction of perusing your excellent pamphlet.

I remain, with great respect and regard, your friend and obedient servant,

EDWARD BATES.

Hon. Caleb B. Smith, Secretary of Interior—

Your refutation of the sophisteries of Senator Breckenridge's speech is full and conclusive. I trust this reply may have an extended circulation at the present time, as I am sure its perusal by the *people* will do much to aid the cause of the Constitution and the Union.

GLOBE OFFICE, *August* 8, 1861.

Allow me to thank you for the privilege of reading your admirable review of Mr. Breckenridge's speech. I have enjoyed it greatly. Especially have I been struck with its very ingenious and just exposition of the constitutional law, bearing on the President, assailed by Mr. B., and with the very apt citation of Mr. Jefferson's opinion as to the propriety and necessity of disregarding mere legal punctillio, when the source of all is in danger of destruction. The gradual development of the plot in the South to overthrow the Union is also exceedingly well depicted and with remarkable clearness. If spoken in the Senate your article would have been regarded by the country as a complete and masterly refutation of Mr. B.'s heresies. Though the peculiar position of the Globe might preclude the publication of the review, I am glad that it has not been denied to the editor of the Globe to enjoy what the Globe itself has not been privileged to contain.

I remain, with great respect, your obedient servant,

SAM'L T. WILLIAMS.

In the House of Representatives, on the 22d of January, 1862, Hon. A. S. Diven, of New York, said:

A specious argument in favor of what may be done under the war power by way of confiscation has been made. * * * Any one who desires to see it answered will find that a clever woman has done it completely. * * * The same one, in her cleverness, has answered my friend from Ohio, [Mr. Bingham.]

A MEMBER. What is her name?

Mr. DIVEN. She signs herself, in her pamphlet, Anna Ella Carroll. I commend her answer on the doctrine of the *War Power* to those who have been following that phantom and misleading the people; and I commend it to another individual, a friend of mine, who gave a most learned disquisition on the writ of *habeas corpus* and against the power of the President to imprison men. He will find that answered. I am not surprised at this. The French revolution discovered great political minds in some of the French women, and I am happy to see a like development in our women.

Judge Diven subsequently addressed the following letter to your memorialist:

WASHINGTON, *February* 9, 1862.

I thank you for the note of the 6th. Your pamphlet I have read with satisfaction, as I had your former publication. I have no desire to appear complimentary, but cannot forbear the expression of my admiration of your writings. There is a cogency in your argument that I have seldom met with. Such maturity of judicial learning with so comprehensive and concise a style of communication, surprises me. Ladies have certainly seldom evinced ability as jurists—it may be because the profession was not their sphere—but you have satisfied me that at least one might have been a distinguished lawyer. Go on, madam, in aiding the cause to which you have devoted your talent; your country needs the labor of all her defenders. If the time will ever come when men will break away from passion and return to reason, your labors must be appreciated. Unless that time soon arrives, alas for this Republic! I have almost despaired of the wisdom of men. God's ways are mysterious, and my trust in Him is left me as a ground of hope. I have the honor to be, madam,

Your odedient servant,

A. S. DIVEN.

Hon. Richard S. Coxe, on the 15th of May, 1862, said :

I have never read an abler or more conclusive paper than your " War Power" document in all my reading. Your charges are very reasonable.

WASHINGTON, *May* 22, 1862.

I most cheerfully endorse the papers respecting your publications under the authority of the War Department. Mr. Richard S. Coxe, I can say, is one of the ablest lawyers in this District or in the country. In his opinion of your writings I entirely concur, as with other men who have expressed one. I regret I am without the influence to serve you at the War Department, but Mr. Lincoln, with whom I have conversed, has, I know, the highest appreciation of your services in this connection. Judge Collamer, whom I regard as among the first of living statesmen and patriots, is enthusiastic in praise of your publications, and indeed I have heard but one opinion expressed by all the able men who have referred to them.

Sincerely yours,

R. J. WALKER.

P. S.—I expect shortly to control a *monthly*, where your contributions will ever find a welcome place, especially in connection with the war.

Hon. Edgar Cowan, U. S. Senator from Greensburg, Pa., 11th September, 1862, wrote:

* * * I am ignorant of the value in money of the articles in question. I believe they were eminently useful and ought to be paid for fully.

Hon. Reverdy Johnson said:

From the opinions of able men, in whose judgment I have all confidence, your charges are moderate.

Hon. Charles O'Conor, of the New York bar, on the 10th of October, 1862, said:

Without intending to express any assent or dissent to the positions therein asserted, but merely with a view of forming a judgment in respect to their merits as argumentative compositions, I have carefully perused Miss Carroll's pamphlets. The propositions are clearly stated, the authorities relied on are judiciously selected, and the reasoning is natural, direct, and well sustained, and framed in a manner extremely well adapted to win the reader's assent, and thus to obtain the object in view. I consider the charges quite moderate.

Hon. Edward Everett, on the 20th of September, 1862, said:

I distinctly recollect that I thought them written with very great ability and research, and as Miss Carroll has unquestionably performed her part of the agreement with fidelity and a truly patriotic spirit, that of the Department, I have no doubt, will be fulfilled with liberality.

Hon. William M. Meredith, of Pennsylvania, on the 4th of October, 1862, said:

I had the pleasure of reading the publication on the War Powers of the Government, and it certainly exhibits very great ability and research.

Hon. Horace Binney, sr., of Philadelphia, in October, 1862, said:

No publications evoked by the war have given me greater pleasure. They exhibit great ability and patient investigation, and the pamphlet on the War Powers of the Government has the additional merit of being in advance of any similar one, and rendered a timely and valuable service to the country.

Hon. Jacob Collamer, late United States Senator, December 5, 1862, said:

There can be no question of the great intellectual value of these productions, or of their eminent usefulness to the cause of the Union. Were I Secretary of War I would cheerfully pay every dollar charged.

Ex-Governor Hicks, of Maryland, then United States Senator, February 5, 1863, said:

I know if Secretary Stanton could give his attention to your business matter it would be settled to your satisfaction; for he could not express himself stronger than he has done to me of your services to the country. And President Lincoln has talked of you to me several times in the same way, and so have many of the ablest Unionists in Congress.

I said at the War Department to Mr. Watson that I did not pretend to be competent to judge of the money value of literary performances, but I could say that your writings had had a powerful influence in Maryland for good, and that your defense of the war and the administration of Mr. Lincoln did more of itself to elect a Union man as my successor than all the rest of the campaign documents put together.

As you know, I am ready to serve you in any way I possibly can. Your moral and material support I shall never forget, in that trying ordeal, such as no other man in this country ever went through.

GREENSBURG, PA., *May* 3, 1873.

Miss Carroll: * * * I do remember well that Mr. Lincoln expressed himself in wonder and admiration at your papers upon the proper course to be pursued in legislating for the crisis. * * * In this connection I know that he considered your opinions sound and coming from a lady most remarkable for their knowledge of international and constitutional law.

EDGAR COWAN.

Rev. Dr. Breckenridge on the 6th of December, 1864, in referring to the part performed in the civil war by himself and your memorialist, writes:

* * * Is it not a purer, perhaps a higher ambition, to prove that in the most frightful times and through long years a single citizen had it in his power, by his example, his voice and his pen—by courage, by disinterestedness, by toil, to become a real power in the State of himself, which no power beside could wholly disregard. And have not you delicately nurtured women as you are, also *cherished a similar ambition and done a similar work even from a more difficult position.* * * It gives me great pleasure to learn that you propose to publish annals of this revolution, and I trust you will be spared to execute that purpose.

Your friend and servant,

R. J. BRECKINRIDGE.

DANVILLE, KY.

Your memorialist will now state that it is conclusively shown in the foregoing pages that *the plan for opening the Mississippi and destroying the rebel power in the Southwest*, was submitted to the Government in November, 1861, as set forth in her memorial.

2. That the armies advanced along the *line of the Tennessee river to the decisive position on the Memphis and Charleston railroad* as pointed out in the plan and by consequence the Mississippi was opened and the power of the rebellion effectually broken.

3. That Assistant Secretary of War, Thomas A. Scott, through whom the plan was submitted, and President Lincoln and Secretary Stanton, by whom the campaign was inaugurated, *recognized your memorialist as its author, and awarded to her its merit.*

4. That the pamphlets published under the auspices of the War Department were of great value to the Government, and her charges were moderate, and should have been *fully paid.*

5. That your memorialist gave her time and energies exclusively to the cause of the Union throughout the struggle, and *it was understood* by the Assistant Secretary of War, Colonel Scott, as well as by your memorialist, *that the Gov-*

ernment should treat her with sufficient liberality to compensate her for any service she might render.

Your memorialist respectfully asks you to make the service she rendered the people and Government of the United States the basis of your action, and reward her somewhat in proportion to the benefits received.

ANNA ELLA CARROLL.

MARCH 28, 1874.

APPENDIX 1.

EXTRACTS FROM THE DEBATES IN CONGRESS IN 1861-62 ON THE MILITARY SITUATION—THE TENNESSEE CAMPAIGN—PREVENTING FINANCIAL BANK- RUPTCY, AND FOREIGN INTERVENTION.

IN THE HOUSE OF REPRESENTATIVS.

DECEMBER 16, 1861.

Mr. WICKLIFFE: One thing I do know that whenever your army moves take possession of Columbus, a position seized and fortified, since the adjournment of the last Con- gress, you will require every soldier that can be brought to bear to take *that* place, and make an advance down the Mississippi river. When the army moves with the view of carrying out the plan of campaign, I do not want that we shall have to leave one tenth of its force behind to protect the base of its operations in this campaign. And the first decisive battle that is to be fought in this campaign against the rebel army, *will be fought on Kentucky soil.*

Mr. MORRILL: If the people are willing to furnish 20,000 more men to put down this rebellion I say let us bid them God speed in the work. We know there is necessity for a very large force in that State. There is a large Confederate army at Columbus, and another at Bowling Green. We know that under Zollicoffer, Kentucky is invaded through. Cumberland Gap and   *   *   Humphrey Marshall is in another direction.

Mr. MAYNARD: Kentucky occupies a peculiar situation in connection with our public affairs. * * She is not only invaded by armies in large force and great strength, but she has the elements of disorder within her own borders. She is surrounded by hostile forces on three sides who wish to make her union and loyal citizens feel the full force of their wrath. * * Hence she is subject to invasion from these quarters. * * You want men familiar with the country, who have that sort of local knowledge to enable them to meet this invading insurrectionary force.

Mr. BLAIR : We see the fact plainly as the Administration can see it, that our armes *are not advancing*, and that we have never met the enemy except when the enemy was in an overwhelming superior numbers.

Mr. RICHARDSON : The misfortune that has attended us heretofore has been that *we have not been familiar with the country where we have to fight.* * * Our base of operations has got to be Louisville.

Mr. DIVEN : This rebellion must be put down speedily or it will wear out the resources of the country. * * * Let it be made apparent that by an additional force in Kentucky, this rebellion can be put down *one month* sooner. No better economy can be employed than by the expenditure of this money in Kentucky. Suppose it will be $10,000,000 or $20,000,000, and that it will end the rebellion *one month sooner*, why we will then save $30,000,000, for I believe the current expenses of the Government are $30,000,000 per month.

The question with me is, whether granting this increase of appropriation will hasten *one hour* the crushing of the rebellion ?

Mr. WRIGHT : If the great battle which is to determine the question whether the Government is to exist or not, is to be fought in Kentucky or in the vicinity of Kentucky, I think the time may come when we shall be very glad to avail ourselves of this force raised by Kentucky. * * The rebellion has now assumed such formidable proportions we must call it war—that is its proper and legitimate name * * * and in its *issue* is involved the cause of freedom and the power of man for self government.

Mr. CONWAY : The report of the Secretary of Treasury tells a fearful tale. Nearly two millions a day will hardly suffice to cover our existing expenditures. Eight hundred thousand strong men in the prime of life are abstracted from the laboring population to consume and be a tax on those who remain to work. * * Up to this time we have not encountered the enemy in a single engagement of importance in which we have had an unquestioned victory.

Mr. THADEUS STEVENS : I confess I do not see how, unless the expenses are greatly curtailed, *this Government can pos-*

sibly go on over six months. If we go on * * * **as** we are doing * * * the finances, not only of the Government, but of the whole country, must give way, and the people will be involved in one general bankruptcy and ruin.

Mr. CRITTENDEN: We are engaged now in the *greatest war the world ever saw* * * * The fall of the Roman empire was *nothing* to the civilization of the world *in comparison* with the preservation of this great Union. * * * *Men were never intrusted with such an issue as we are.* * * * All other policies are insignificant in comparison with the rescue of our country from the perils which surround it on every side. * * * Make sure you give us and our posterity a homestead, before you talk about the smaller policies. * * * *Your homestead is in question today, mine, the national existence.*

IN THE SENATE.
DEC. 17, 1861.

MR. LANE, *of Kansas:* I do not wish to risk a battle with inferior numbers—but a battle with equal or superior numbers, a well contested bloody battle we must fight. This war cannot draw its slow length along until Spring. There must be a *decisive stroke within the next few weeks.* Gain a victory before England send her armies and navies upon us, and *England will not send that navy nor these armies.* It is a victory we want and a victory we must have.

Mr. GRIMES: This war is exceedingly oppressive upon that section of country in which I have the honor to reside. We are the only people of the loyal States that feels this war *oppressively.* The result is there is no money in the Northwest.

Mr. BROWNING: We are probably on the *very verge of a* rupture with one of the most powerful nations of the earth, whose power is to be united with the rebels in their fierce struggle against us. .

IN THE HOUSE.
DEC. 30, 1861.

Mr. THADEUS STEVENS: We see why certain leading journals in England sympathize with the South and suggest means to evade the blockade and kindly advise us *to settle peaceably* with the rebels. * I doubt not she will use every means in her power to open the Southern ports. The most surprising thing is the impertinent interference of France.

JANUARY 7, 1862.

Mr. DIVENS: The enemies of this Government began long since to prepare the way for their success. * * They labored to create prejudices against us in Europe. They had their emissaries in every capitol of Europe to instil into the minds of the *merchants* and *manufactures* and *traders* there, the necessity in case of a separation, of their siding with the South and to show them the *great advantage* of opening the Southern ports to free trade with them—and thus the commercial and trading mind of Europe was prepared and its sympathies were years ago enlisted on the side of the South in *this* struggle, that they have been secretly bringing upon the country. The seed thus sewn had grown, and the commercial mind of England had a strong attachment to the South, and strong expectations from the South. That state of feeling existing, every circumstance that was calculated to provoke them against the North would be seized upon and the most would be made of it.

Mr. KELLEY: I think our whole course of action or rather *inaction* invites them to declare war. * * I think the condition of this Capitol to-day invites war. It is environed within a narrow circle of two hundred thousand men in arms. And yet, sir, that short river which leads to the Capitol of a great and proud country, thus defended and encircled by patriot troops is so thoroughly blockaded by rebels, that the Government, though its army has not an adequate supply of forage, cannot bring upon it a peck of oats to feed a hungry horse. * * Call it what you may it is a sight at which men may well wonder.

We have six hundred thousand men in the field.

We have spent I know not how many millions of dollars and *what have we done?* What *one evidence of determined war or military skill have we exhibited to foreign nations or to our own people?* * * We have been engaged in war for seven months. * * England *does* respect power. * * Let her hear the shouts of a victorious army * * and England and the powers of the continent will pause with bated breath.

Sir, it was said yesterday the last day had come; * * my

heart has felt the *last day of our dear country was rapidly approaching.* Before we have achieved a victory *we have reached bankruptcy.* We are to-day flooding the country with an irredeemable currency. In ninety days, with the patriotism of the people paralyzed by the inaction of our great army; * * the funded debt of the country will depreciate with a rapidity that will startle us. In ninety days more, * * the nations of the world will, I fear, be justified in saying to us: " You have no more right to shut up the cotton fields of the world by a vain and fruitless endeavor to reconquer the territory now in rebellion than China or Japan has to wall themselves in." And in the eyes of international law, in the eyes of the world, and I fear in the eyes of impartial history they will be *justified* in breaking our blockade and giving to the rebels means and munitions of war. * * But, sir, in *less than ninety days* to come, back to the point of time, we shall be advancing in the month of April when Northern men will begin to feel the effects of heat in the neighborhood of Ship Island and the mouth of the Mississippi. Looking at the period of ninety days, I say it is not a double but a triple-edged sword approaching, perhaps, the single thread of destiny upon which the welfare of our country hangs. Bankruptcy and miasmetic pestilence are sure to come with the lapse of that period, and *foreign* war may add its horrors to theirs.

Mr. WRIGHT: We are gasping for life. This great Government is upon the brink of a volcano which is heaving to and fro, and we are *not certain whether we exist or not.*

Mr. F. A. CONCKLING: In this crisis of our history when the very existence of the Republic is threatened, when in all human probability the *next thirty days* will decide forever whether the Union is to maintain its place among the powers of the earth, or whether it is to go down and constitutional liberty is to perish. * * At this time it does appear to me that every effort should be made to economize the energies of the Treasury.

IN THE SENATE.

Mr. WILSON *of Mass.:* Why, sir, you can be borne all over this country upon a wave of popular murmur against the Government at this time, and I must say, too, in regard to the men controlling the civil and military affairs of the country. * * It springs from that *deep disappointment of the people* of the country, who have poured out five hundred thousand men, and hundreds of millions of dollars, and who see *no results.* They see no policy in the Administration of the country, *they see no plans—they read of no victories.*

IN THE HOUSE.

JANUARY 13, 1862.

Mr. DAWES: Mr. Speaker, it takes $2,000,000 *every day* to support the army in the field. One hundred millions have thus been expended, since we met here in December, upon an army in *repose.* What they will be when that great day shall arrive when our eyes may be gladdened with the sight of the army in action I do not know. * * What it may cost to put down this rebellion I care very little provided it may be put down. * * * When the history of these times shall have been written, it will be doubtful on whom the guilt will rest most heavily, *upon him who conspired to destroy, or upon him who has proved incompetent to preserve the institutions bequeathed to us by our fathers.* * * * Amid all these things, is it strange the public Treasury trembles and staggers like a strong man with a great burden upon him?

Sir, *that man beneath an exhausted receiver, gasping for breath, is not more helpless to-day than the Treasury of this Government.* * * * Without income from your custom-houses, from your land sales, from any source whatever, to sustain the Treasury notes you are now issuing, they are already beginning to fall in the market. Already they are sold at five per cent. discount at the tables of the money-changers—six per cent. my friend near me says. * * * *Sixty days of the present state of things will bring about a consummation.* It is impossible for the Treasury of the United States to meet this state of things *sixty days longer,* and an *ignominious peace is upon this country and at our very doors.*

JANUARY 14, 1862.

Mr. JULIAN: In the opinion of many the great model republic of the world is in *the throes of death.* This is one of the grand judgment days of history. * * Mr. Seward in his letter to Mr. Clay, of May 6th, admits that *"the object of this rebellion is to create a nation built upon the principle that African* *slavery is a blessing, to be extended over this continent at whatever sacrifice."* * * We are still in eminent peril of foreign war. * * What is it that has called into deadly conflict from the walks of peace, more than a million of men, brethren and kindred, and the joint heirs of a common heritage of liberty. * * The solemn *issue of life and death* must be disposed of upon its merits. * * In the beginning neither the Administration nor the people foresaw the magnitude of this struggle.

JANUARY 15, 1862.

Mr. MORRILL: Unless we propose to ignominiously back down from the vigorous prosecution of the war, every man I suppose in this House will vote in favor of the resolution. This resolution is to assure the country which has an *impatience* what is becoming *chronic*, that whatever the army may be doing, the Committee of Ways and Means have not hutted nor gone into winter quarters.

Mr. WADSWORTH: There are two dangers which threaten the Union. One is a *foreign* war—the other *dissensions among its friends* * * Foreign war would possibly secure the present position of the rebellious States. * * Its worst effect would be to fix their boundaries where they now stand. * *

Mr. CAMPBELL: How long will it be, in the judgment of this House, before a hostile foe will strike at the commerce of this country on the high seas? * * How long will it be before she attempts to drive our commerce from the ocean?

Mr. CRITTENDEN: We are guarding against a foreign war by these appropriations. * * We have a more formidable and more important war. * * It is waged in the heart of the country, and the *life of the country depends upon it.* * * We have not money enough to carry on the war * * which demands of us the defense of our country and our whole government.

Mr. LOVEJOY: Nothing in the future, if we can prophecy that which will come to pass and from indications of the present, than that we *shall* need protection against foreign powers.

JANUARY 20, 1862.

Mr. WRIGHT: There is one great abiding and powerful issue to-day, and that is the issue *whether the country and the Constitution shall be saved, or whether it shall be utterly and entirely annihilated.* With Pennsylvania it is a question of national existence of life or death. * * The great heart of Pennsylvania is beating to-day for the cause of the Union ; * * it is to *decide* the great question, whether the liberty which has been handed down to us by our fathers shall be permitted to remain in the land, or whether chaos and desolation shall blot out the country and Government forever.

IN THE SENATE.
JANUARY 22, 1862.

Mr. WADE: But, sir, though the war lies dormant, still there is war, and it is not intended that it shall remain in this quiescent state *much longer.* The committee to which I have the honor to belong are determined * * that it *shall move and move with energy.* If Congress will not give us or give themselves power to act with efficiency in war, we must confide everything to the Executive Government, and let them usurp everything, if you would not fix your machinery so that you might advise with me and act with me, * * * I would act independent of you, and you might call it what you please.

This is for the suppression of the rebellion, and the measures that we are to sit in *secrecy* upon look to that *end* and none other. No measure rises in importance above that connected with the suppression of this rebellion. * * We stand here for the people, and we act for them. * * There is no danger to be apprehended from any *secrecy* which, in the consideration of war measures, we may deem it proper to adopt. *It is as proper for us as it is for the general in the field,* as it is for your Cabinet ministers to discuss matters in secret when they pertain to war.

Mr. GARRETT DAVIS : Secession now has reduced your Republic, its power, its character, and its moral influence to *contempt* all over the world. *This Government is struggling for its existence—it is a life and death struggle,* whether its laws be executed or not. * * The people will give their blood and their lives to carry on this war, longer than they will give their money, but will eventually become tired of both contributions. * * *No man has been able to say whether to-morrow's sun would shine upon the re-establishment or the dissolution of the Union,* and whether the Government would ever rally the energy, and power, and means, and men enough to reconstruct it.

IN THE HOUSE.

JANUARY 22, 1862.

Mr. THADEUS STEVENS : The enemies of free Government predicted with the utmost confidence the overthrow of this Union by internal dissensions. * Eighty years of unexampled prosperity seemed to belie their predictions. We were establishing on a firm basis the great truths proclaimed by our fathers. * * If we meet and conquer in this dreadful issue, it will produce benefits which will *compensate* for all it costs. *It will give to this nation centuries of peace, and constitutional freedom.* * * They have a *vast* country to overrun. * * Every means in the power of nature must be exhausted before our sacred duty is abandoned. * * *If the Government submits it * * loses its character and ceases to be a power among the nations of the earth.* * * If no other means were left to save the Republic, I believe we have the power * * to declare a *dictator* without confining our choice to any officer of the Government. Rather than the nation should perish, I would do it. Rather than see the Union dissolved—nay, rather than see one star stricken from its banner—I would do it *now.* * * Remember that *every day's delay* costs the nation $1,500,000 and hundreds of lives. * * What an *awful* responsibility rests upon those in authority. Their *mistakes* may bring mourning upon the land and sorrow to many a fireside. * * "If we cannot save our honor, save at least the *lives* and *treasure* of the nation."

IN THE SENATE.

JANUARY 28, 1862.

Mr. WILSON, of Mass. : We have assembled large armies. It is expected that these armies are to *move.* The public voice *demands action.* They have to move over large spaces of country; railways must be a great means of transportation for them. * * The object is to concentrate our forces * * without the knowledge or consent of anybody, or letting these troops know where they are to go, or how many are to go. * * The purpose of the Government in wishing to have power over the railways of the country is, to be enabled to move the armies of the United States during the *next few months*; * * to move them by the will of the Government, in such numbers as it pleases and where it pleases. * *

Mr. Wade: The Secretary of War does not want to take possession of these railroads permanently, but for certain expeditions, to give energy to the Department, to give efficiency to the cause. * * One of our undoubted powers is to seize all the railroads in this nation if the Government wants them for transportation of troops and munitions of war. * * All I want is to regulate by law that power the Executive already has. * * Look at the complaints against the President because he has undertaken to suspend the *habeas corpus.* * * I justify the President in all he has done, because he acted from an *over willing necessity.*

Mr. Garrett Davis: I have in my imagination fancied this Union subsisting for a thousand years, extending through the centuries that numbered the history of Carthage, of Rome, and of the modern kingdoms of France and England. It was to me the most grievous disappointment * * that this Union in the first century after the foundation of the Government it should be broken up. * * I still cherish the hope that we shall *bring back* this Union, and place it upon the firm foundation it occupied before these Southern discontents rocked it to its basis.

IN THE HOUSE.

JANUARY 28, 1862.

Mr. Spalding: *We were never in greater peril than this moment.* * * But, sir, I will not, I dare not, I hope none of us will shrink from the responsibility of performing every duty devolved on us in this great *crisis* of our national affairs. The bill before us is a war measure—a measure of *necessity* and not of choice * * to meet the most pressing demands upon the Treasury to sustain the army and navy until they can make a *vigorous* advance * * and crush the rebellion * * extraordinary means must be resorted to, in order to save our Government and preserve our nationality. * * This bill is a Government measure. * * By the time the Secretary of the Treasury can get these notes engraved, printed and signed ready for use, all other means at his command and in the Treasury will be *exhausted.* This measure then is presented under the highest prerogative of the Government.

The army and navy now in the service must be *paid.* They must be supplied with food, clothing, arms, ammunition, and all other material of war, to render them effective. * Having exhausted other means of sustaining the Government this measure is brought as the best that can be devised in the present exigency to relieve the necessities of the Treasury. * * With the enormous expenditures of the Government, to pay the extraordinary expenses of the war,* * *the Treasury must be supplied from some source or the Government must stop payment in a very few days.* * * A loan put upon the market in the present depressed state of the United States stocks, to be followed by other large loans, is not regarded as a favorable mode of maintaining the Goverment at the present time. * * The situation of the country is now different from what it was *two months ago.* The circumstances have changed, and the Secretary and Congress will find it necessary to conform their action to what *can* be done and not what they would like to do were it otherwise practicable. * * With a navy and army of six hundred thousand men in the field, requiring with the other expenses of the Government an average daily expenditure of more than $1,600,000. This new system of banking will not afford the relief in *time* to enable the Secretary to meet the pressing demands made upon him. * * The tables from the Census Bureau shows that the true value of the property, real and personal, within the United States is $16,000,000,000, * * this is the capital on which your treasury notes and bonds rest. * * Congress is clothed with this mighty power to sustain the nation at this time. * * The exercise of the power is an *imperative* necessity in order to sustain the credit of the nation at this time. * * *The life of the nation is in peril,* and all that we *have,* and all that we *hope for* must be devoted to maintain its existence. * * An *early* and *successful advance of our armies is of the utmost importance ;* we need such an advance to *sustain the financial credit of the Government ; we need it to prevent foreign intervention ; we need it to rouse the flagging energies of the people,* and above all, we need it to vindicate the courage and invincibility of our brave soldiers.

Mr. SHEFFIELD: It requires our coolest, ripest judgment to consider the means to put down this rebellion. * * Popular government is now on *trial,* and in its success is involved the maintenance of the Union. It would be better, far better that every loyal man at the North should be slain than that this rebellion should not be suppressed.

The generations of future centuries will look back to this period of our history and calculate the *effect* of our conduct upon *human civilization.* * * It is a matter of consequence to the civilized world, not only the men of this generation but to the men of all future times, that this *Government* should not be overthrown. Our people desire it to be put down. They would sooner have *all their property consumed* and every man *slain* on the *battle field* * * than submit to this lawless power of rebel hosts.

JANUARY 29, 1862.

Mr. GURLEY: When a *few more months* have gone by it would be no strange thing if the Southern Confederacy should be acknowledged by foreign powers, and when that takes place, if ever, our Government will stand before the civilized world, not only humiliated, but utterly disgraced. * * If we would have the moral support of this world, we must strike boldly for victory. * * Remember this contest must close, either in the ruin of a Republic that has filled the eyes of the best men of the world with admiration, and possibly the destruction of civil and religious liberty in America, * * or in the renewed stability of our cherished institutions. * * *Our army has been five months getting ready for its realization.* * * The people everywhere are imploring for and demanding active movements against the rebels in the South. * * Sir, it is a *serious question with many honest minds, whether this Congress and Government, and this great nation are not to-day sleeping upon a volcano,* Murmurs deep and strong are *everywhere* coming up from the people against the inaction of our army.

* * Meanwhile the public Treasury is being drained for their support; the *fleets of three powerful nations are nearing our shores,* and if our military do not rouse themselves to speedy action, * * these fleets may make a visit to our Southern coasts * * and announce to us that *cotton* is an absolute necessity in Europe, and the blockade must continue no longer.

* * All this is not only possible but in the contingency of continued inactivity * * *highly probable.* But * * the new Secretary of War, a man who, if report speaks truly, is like brave Ben. Wade of Ohio, a good combination of old Hickory and Zack Taylor * * will push on the war with all the vigor that characterized the people in raising so vast, so mighty an army.

JANUARY 30, 1862.

Mr. S. S. Cox: General McClellan intended first to have General Buell get the Tennessee railroad; that for this end he has given all his energies to aid him. * * When General Buell took command he found his troops straggling and scattered. He had to gather them and concentrate and form them into regiments. * * I speak *knowingly* when I declare to this Congress and the people that no delay of Gen. Buell's movements are attributable to any orders from Gen. McClellan—on the contrary he has ordered him * * not to lose a day or an hour in the accomplishment of the design to seize the Tennessee railroad, to the end that not only shall Eastern Tennessee be opened to the army and Union * * but to the grand aim to cut off this rebel army of the Potomac, not alone from the line of their supplies, but from the line of their retreat. * * In fear for the fate of *Memphis,* Gen. Beauregard is hurried out to Columbus, Kentucky, to avert the Northern avalanche which impends there, while Buell is drawing with consummate skill his fatal line around the confederates, as the lines have been drawn in Virginia. * * Thousands of our people now regard with *dampened spirit* and *sad silence the condition of our country, and they are almost dismayed by our terrible presel nd still more unpropitious future.* But what * * if the masses of the Union are to be quenched? We shall lose our place among the nations, our relative importance on the globe, our physical independence, our weight in the equilibrium of powers, our frontiers, alliances, and geography. * * * These make up the immortality of a nation. * * He who remains silent when such interests are at stake is treacherous to his land and to his God.

JANUARY 31, 1862.

Mr. Sargent: Had not the Trent embroglio admitted of a peaceful solution, * * this day, as we sit here, the first blow would have been struck (by Great Britain) and the harbor of San Francisco sealed. * * To-day we are trying to provide means to pay, or secure to be paid, a debt of $1,000,000,000 on account of this war, of which we have but just commenced the first campaign. * * The hostile feeling towards this country which seized upon the late trivial affair *still exists,* and I say here that there is danger of a war until * * England is incapable of giving or we of receiving an insult.

FEB. 3, 1862.

M. WICKLIFFE : Look, sir, at the condition of Kentucky at the beginning of this session. * * Do we know how soon General Thomas will make an assault upon *Bowling Green*? He will be obliged to leave a part of his army at every gap upon his line to prevent his rear being annoyed or cut off from communications. We want men from our own State. They know the fastnesses of the mountains. They know all the country, and will be better guards there than any others. * * We have information that General Beauregard and fifteen thousand of his trained bands have gone to Kentucky to unite with the forces now there, against us.

FEBRUARY 4, 1862.

Mr. BINGHAM : Unless the people can, and will stand by the national credit and sustain it by such overwhelming majorities as to silence opposition, then the experiment of free representative Government must melt in the thin air. * * The nation's credit cannot be maintained by *force* unless the majority of the people with whom are the issues of the nation's life, voluntarily acquiesce in any and all needful legislation.

Mr. ROSCOE CONKLING : I was saying what the people must know about the use of their money. * * They simply want to know that the people's servants are using the people's money and the nation's army to hurl swift destruction upon the nation's foes. * * Unless we appeal to the monied interest of the country with an adequate policy we can get no money, we ought not get it, we shall not deserve it.

Debts funded or liquidated up to Jan. '62,	$306,000,000
The floating debt, ...	200,000,000
The required ordinary and extraordinary, to July 1, ...	300,000,000
	$806,000,000

This last item is at the rate of $2,000,000 *per day* for one hundred and fifty days. If $45,000,000 a month is taken as a estimate, it will be $225,000,000. * * The Secretary of War says, that 718,512 men have taken the field. * * Every one of this multitude of soldiers is entitled to at least thirteen dollars beside subsistence and bounties. * * There has been no such occasion presented, *no such demand made upon a nation during the life time of the human race.* The history of free Government, the history of America, the history of *Constitutional Liberty, begins or ends now.* * * Our destiny is, without an ally in the world, with the nations *banded against us* to hold fast a continent in the midst of the greatest, guiltiest revolution the world has ever seen.

Mr. PIKE: Who knows what course this business shall take in the next *ninety days?* With us here, it is a matter of guess work. We are the money partners in this Government concern. * * Still nobody is allowed to know any thing about it. * * If the *plan* shadowed forth by the gentleman from Ohio [Mr. Cox.] who spoke * * for the commanding general is really to be adopted, the sooner we supply ourselves with the money we want the better for the Treasury. * * The "Anaconda" scheme * * is to surround cut off communications with the world, and wait the result. In the meantime disease is wasting our noble army, and uneasiness is increasing in every portion of the loyal States. * * The Secretary of War on whom the *country now leans* with entire confidence, I trustingly believe that his strong will and clear head shall prove sufficient * * *in this time of great distress.* * * The army *will* respond with enthusiasm and *victories* which are the best *financiers* in these days, will be the happy result. * * The next *sixty days are to be the nations opportunity* to reassert itself.

Mr. WRIGHT: What is humiliating to me is that the credit of the nation is not able to make loans of money from foreign countries. *It cannot be done.* * * I do not think there is any government in Europe that we can expect to make any advance to us in a loan to carry on the war. * * We must rely solely on our own element of strength and power. * * The question of liberty itself is at stake. * * When the people *see* that something is to be done, they will furnish their money to the Government as readily as they have their men. * * I think the indications are, especially at the War Department, that something will be done. * * I am sorry to say it, but there has been a *gradual* WEAKENING of the faith of the people. * * I want something done to convince the people that the Administration are in earnest, and *has a definite plan which it has to work out.* * * The time for mysterious utterances about a movement that is in the wind, or seen or heard or whispered, and gave a little hope at the time, is passed by. * * I do not think the Secretary of the Treasury, when he goes to New York, will say * * there is to be a great movement within such a time, and inspire the bankers with the hope that the good time is coming within fifteen days, * * but the people want *action* in the Administration in the military department of the Government. * * How and when and the mode, I say nothing about, but there *must be action* everywhere. * * The people will then become inspired with the belief that the rebellion will be put down before harvest, and they will pour out their *money* like water.

IN THE SENATE.

FEBRUARY 4, 1862.

Mr. MORRILL: Well, sir, is the Senate prepared to-day to say that it will enter upon an enterprise, enter upon the construction of mail-clad steamers designed for the prosecution of this war, to have a bearing simply upon this rebellion, which are not to be completed for the next twelve months? Sir, if this whole thing is not brought to an end in the next *six months the nation will be beyond the hope of relief.*

Mr. GRIMES: You all know that Great Britian has now the *Warrior* and *Hero* ready for use. We were told a little while ago, that the Warrior was coming to our coast—a large *immense frigate* which according to naval authorities is a complete success, and preparations have been made for building a great many more.

FEBRUARY 5, 1862.

Mr. SHERMAN: It is manifest that the people of this country will be called upon to bear an amount of not less than $700,000,000. * * This is more than *four* times the aggregate currency of the country—it is more than the government of Great Britain bore in her struggle with Napoleon. * * It is more than any country in *ancient* or *modern times* has *attempted to carry.* There is nothing like it in history. * * No nation ever attempted it or approached it, never for any length of time.

FEBRUARY 6, 1862.

Mr. Sherman: That this condition of affairs is exciting attention abroad and at home is true. I have here an extract from a recent English paper, in which they speak of this very condition of affairs. Our friends across the water are now looking into all our deficiencies, and all our difficulties. Here is a remarkable statement from the government organ, said to be owned by Lord Palmerston:

"The monetary intelligence from America is of the most important kind, national bankruptcy is not an agreeable prospect, but it is the only one presented by the *existing state of American finance."*

"What a strange tale does the history of the United States in the past twelve months unfold. What a striking moral does it not point. Never before was the world dazzled by a career of more reckless extravagance. Never before did a flourishing and prosperous State make such gigantic strides toward effecting its *own* ruin."—*London Post, January* 15, 1862.

And you all have probably read the recent extract in the *"London Times"* in which our country is denounced in the most unmitigated language that is too offensive to be read in the Senate.

I merely quote these matters to show you that our *financial condition* has attracted the attention of foreign governments. It is an element of weakness, and they count upon it in all the political questions that will arise in the *next sixty or ninety days,* or the next year. They look at this vast expenditure *as a dangerous element as a reason why we cannot succeed* in *this contest,* and as a reason why they should *interfere* in it. * * I do not show these facts which are plain and palpable on their face, in order to impair our public credit. What I state is *known* to every money lender in this land. There is not a bank or a broker who does not know these facts as well as I do. I do not do it for the purpose of stopping the prosecution of the war. * * Indeed I cannot contemplate the condition of my country, if it shall be dissevered and divided. Take the loyal States as they now stand, and look at the map of the United States, and regard two hostile confederacies stretching along for two thousand miles across the continent. * * Do you not know the normal condition of such a state of affairs would be eternal war, everlasting war. Two nations of the same blood, of the same lineage, of the same spirit, cannot occupy the same continent, much less stand side by side as rival nations, dividing rivers and mountains for their boundaries. * * Rather than yield to traitors or the intervention of foreign powers, rather than bequeath to the next generation a broken Union, and an interminable civil war, I would light the torch of fanaticism and destroy all that the labor of the two generations has accumulated. * * *If you can show me the reason by which the present expenditures can be maintained by our national Government*, you show the means to success, to honor, to glory, to the preservation of the Union, and of our Government.

Mr. WILSON *of Mass:* The credit of this Government is *sinking daily under our feet.* * * Why, Mr. President, there was a time, and not far back, when the credit of this Government stood high, when it could command its millions; but to-day, with $40,000,000 due the people, of which the Government is *unable to pay one red cent*, we propose to issue one hundred or one hundred and fifty millions of dollars of paper money and make *that* paper money a legal tender. We are going to spend five or six hundred millions of dollars a year and no one has yet pointed out the way to obtain that money, and it will take a long process to reach it. It is in vain to cry up the credit of this Government, to boast of it, or talk of it, *unless we perform the acts necessary* to sustain and uphold it. If there is one thing, more than another, that we need to show the people of this country, it is, that we are ready to make some sacrifices.

Mr. DAVIS: I understand the Chairman of the Military Committee, Mr. Wilson, to state that the Government is now indebted $40,000,000, and has no means of paying it. I presume the Government will need in the next six months $300,000,000. *The question is, how is the Government to raise this amount of money?* Sir, *you cannot raise $300,000,000 by taxation, and the Government cannot get along without it.*

IN THE HOUSE.

FEBRUARY 6, 1862.

Mr. THADEUS STEVENS: Congress at the extra session authorized the loan of $250,000,000; $100,000,000 of this was taken at seven and three-tenths per cent., and $50,000,000 of six per cent. bonds at a discount of over $5,000,000; $50,000,000 were used in demand notes payable in coin, leaving $50,000,000 undisposed of. Before the banks had paid much of this last loan *they broke down under it and suspended specie payments.* They have continued to pay the loan, not in coin, but in demand notes of the Government, * * but the last was paid yesterday, and on the same day *the banks refused* to receive them. They must now sink to depreciated currency. The remaining $50,000,000 the Secretary has been *unable* to *negotiate,* * * and there is now a floating debt of at least $180,000,000. The Secretary intended to use the balance of this authorized loan in paying it out to creditors in notes of seven and three-tenths; that becoming *known,* they immediately sunk four per cent., and had he persevered, it is believed they would have been down to ten per cent. discount. But even if this could be used, (about $40,000,000,) there would remain due about $90,000,000, the payment of which is urgently demanded. The daily expenses of the Government are now about $2,000,000. To carry us on to the next meeting of Congress would take $600,000,000 more, making, before legislation could be had next session, about $700,000,000 to be provided for. We have already appropriated $350,000,000, making our entire debt $1,050,000,000.

The grave question now is, how can this large amount be raised? The Secretary of the Treasury has used his best efforts to negotiate a loan of but $50,000,000, and *has failed.*

IN THE SENATE.

FEBRUARY 6, 1862.

Mr. TRUMBULL: I will tell you what the people are clamoring for. *They are clamoring for action on the part of your armies.* The Senator from Rhode Island wants to know how to raise money. Give us *victories, tell your generals to advance.*

Gentlemen tell us there is no money and the fault is with Congress. Has not the Government had money? Did we not raise it by the hundreds of millions in July? Have you not had men, hundreds of thousands of them, and has not God Almighty given you a season for operations in the field, such as was never vouchsafed to a people before. * * Taxation will never save your country; but it is the strong arms and stout hearts that you want to put down this rebellion, and, as my friend Mr. Wade says, somebody to lead them.

FEBRUARY 11, 1862.

Mr. FOSTER: I believe, sir, * * that our whole coast, our Atlantic coast, our Lake coast, our Pacific coast would be much better fortified and protected, by moving down the columns of our Army, now lying near the Upper Mississippi and along the Ohio rivers, through the States of Kentucky and Tennessee, and the States South, *victoriously and triumphantly to the Gulf of Mexico.* * * But, sir, if these points are not very soon in possession of the United States forces, * * if we do not take possession of our Southern ports within *thirty or forty days,* we shall need much more than the amount recommended by the Finance Committee to fortify all the exposed portions of our coast. * * *I doubt whether very much more will protect them from foreign attack.* * * Let us move our *armies* * * at the earliest moment we can, and *more them energetically and successfully and these appropriations will not be needed.* * * I think it is demonstrable that Maine is to be better fortified at *New Orleans* than at Portland, Chicago better at *Charleston* than on Lake Michigan, and Newport better at *Savannah* and *Mobile,* than at the mouth of the Narraganset bay. Let us place our armies and unfurl our flag in these Southern cities, and all these points we are solicitous to protect, will be as safe as it is possible for human fortifications to make them. *Without these we have not men enough, nor money enough to defend them against the forces which will speedily threaten them.*

Mr. HOWE: If it is not safe to publish to the country our own calculations as to the importance of different points on our coast, it may not be dangerous to lay before the country the calculations of other powers and other Governments, and I should therefore like to have the Secretary read from the "London Times," which I send to the desk:

Extract from the London Times of January 7, 1862.

"In the event of a renewal of hostilities which were terminated at the treaty of Ghent, * * the command of the water which separates Upper Canada from the Federal territories would be equivalent to a command in the field. * * It will be seen that the matter divides into two periods, of which the first would be the most critical for England. It becomes a question therefore of the greatest importance how this superiority is likely to be determined. * * Up to the month of April next the lakes may be regarded as inaccessible to the sea, and therefore whatever force is created must be created on the spot. * * *As soon, however, as the St. Lawrence is opened there will be an end of our difficulty. We can then pour into the lakes such a fleet of gunboats and other craft as will give us the complete and immediate command of these waters.* Directly the navigation is opened we can send up vessel after vessel without any restriction. * * The Americans would have no such resource. They would have no access to the lakes from the sea, and it would be impossible that they could construct vessels of any considerable power in the interval that would elapse before the ice is broken up. *With the opening of spring the lakes would be ours, and if the mastery of these waters is indeed the mastery of all, we may expect the result with perfect satisfaction.* * * On the whole, therefore, the conclusion seems clear that *three months* hence the field will be all our own, and in the m antime the Americans, if *judiciously encountered, would not be able to do us much harm."*

Mr. HOWE: The fact is apparent from this communication that in case of a war with a maritime power, and especially a war with England, the *Northwest* is that portion of the country which they design as the theatre of military operations. * * Inasmuch as I had just received this extract from an English paper, I deemed it proper to bring the matter to the attention of the Senate, for I deemed *that* one of the most important points to be fortified in the whole country. It defends a portion of the country which is not only the granary of the nation but almost of the world. * *

Mr. GRIMES: I do not believe they could get through the Welland canal before sometime in the middle of May, even if the vessels were all sent before that time. * * But what are we going to do in the *meantime if hostilities actually commenced, or if they were imminent.* * * Are we going to stand by and fold our arms and not take possession of the Welland canal? * * The British Government has sent over into all *the British colonies of North America some thirty thousand men.* * * The Welland canal is only a few miles from our frontier. * * Is it expected that we will not not render it impassible for the British gunboats?

Mr. FESSENDEN: ' * * Does not every one see the position in which we stand towards *foreign* nations. * * It is obvious to every man's mind that we are engaged at present in a war, which in spite of all our endeavors to preserve peace, may bring about a collision with *foreign powers*. If we speak of things at all we must speak of them as *they are*. * * It is not necessarily a threat to anybody, * * because we see that position and recognize it ourselves. * * Sir, while there is no man in the Senate or the country who more strongly desires *peace* with all nations than I do, * * I cannot shut my eyes to the fact * * that such things may happen, * * especially when the *Executive itself has recommended this bill.* * *My honorable friend from Illinois says* * * *our armies ought to do something, that would be the way to raise finances, and that would be the way to fortify the country.* We all know it. * * Sir, it has been said, and it is well to remember, that there *never was such a war as this in the history of the world— there never was one so difficult to carry on—there never was one which extended over so great a territory* upon which so many points were to be defended and so many attacked. * * I look for and believe that the *results* which are to be accomplished EVEN *before many days, will be such as not only to gratify all our hopes, but to astound the world.* * * *Let us wait for them calmly.*

Mr. TRUMBULL: I thought it might be necessary to repeat * * the necessity of more active operations on the part of our army, and I am gratified to know from the Senator that we are to have more active operations, and that we *we are to have movements which will astonish the country and the world.* I rejoice at it, but I believe we may learn something from the past. * * That we have suffered one summer to pass away, and one fall to pass away, and one winter to pass away, at an expense of $500,000,000 to the country, without doing anything. I think it is our duty to see that no more seasons shall come and go without more efficient action.

FEBRUARY 12, 1862.

Mr. HOWE; Either the treasury must be replenished or the war must be abandoned. The war cannot be abandoned. * * The Government is not gambling for empire, it is *defending its own existence.* * * Sir, if this Government lives, if the nation survives the perils which now beset it, every man knows that the stocks of the United States * * will in a few years command a large premium. * * *

I have said that no one can suffer *if the nation survives the struggle in which it is now engaged.* But the statement suggests the possibility that the Government *may not survive.* What then, it may be asked, will become of the *money loaned* and the notes outstanding? I confess my apprehension that *they will all be lost.* That, I apprehend, *will be the case too with notes and money generally,* let who ever will be the maker, let whoever will be the borrower.

Mr. FESSENDEN: We have suffered ourselves in a measure to be *cast down.* Time has come around, * * and everything looks *as favorable to our cause as the heart of man could desire.*

Mr. CHANDLER: From this day forth we can close the war in sixty days by an advance of our armies, and I believe the time has *now arrived when we will advance our armies,* and when the war will be brought to a close within sixty days. * * *The time has arrived when this rebellion is within our grasp.*

IN THE HOUSE.

FEBRUARY 19, 1862.

Mr. POMEROY: Our army, concerning whose seeming inactivity so many unkind words have been spoken on this floor in the past few months, has *practically ended the war.*

Mr. DIVEN: The times are auspicious. * * One good reason urged in favor of that policy was, that the people *were discouraged from want of success in our army. We have now the encouragement of success. Only let the monied men of the country know that the Government is to succeed in putting down the rebellion,* and we will not have to plead for credit. It is not gold and silver that we want. It is not things that are to be *taken* for gold and silver that we want. *It is credit, it is confidence on the part of men who have money to lend, and who can lend it to the Government with the assurance that it will be returned to them.* This is all that is wanted. And now, in view of the *brilliant prospect before us* for a speedy termination of the rebellion, in heaven's name let us leave no national dishonor to remain a stain upon the country.

Mr. GOOCH: The relations of this committee (Conduct of

the War) *with the President, Secretary of War, and all]* the officers of the Cabinet, are of the most cordial nature. * *
Bowling Green, Fort Henry, and Fort Donelson, *are only the beginning of the chapter which is to be the last in the history of this rebellion.* * * If there is any department in which this committee have felt a deeper interest than any other, it is the department in which the gentleman from Kentucky is specially interested.

Mr. ROSCOE CONCKLING : I believe the creation of this committee has been instrumental, with other kindred agencies, in bringing about valuable reforms, which have inaugurated beneficial changes and a *vitalizing policy,* without which we might not have had the victories which *millions to-day applaud.*

IN THE SENATE.

FEBRUARY 24, 1862.

Mr. DOOLITTLE: We go into this struggle with all the energy which God Almighty has given us. The recent victories give earnest of speedy results, but let us rejoice with trembling. The results of battles none but God can foresee. While we have reason to hope that our flag will soon wave at Savannah, at Memphis, at Nashville, and at New Orleans, let us remember we have met reverses before, and let that remembrance chasten our rejoicing.

APRIL 18, 1862.

Mr. HOWARD: Our campaigns have been *planned and carried out by the President, aided by his ordinary advisers and his subordinate military officers.* * * The Government of the United States has witnessed what no monarchy ever witnessed. *It has coped with the most formidable rebellion in the history of world, one which no monarchical government since the dawn of history, could have stood six weeks.*

APRIL 21, 1862.

Mr. COLLAMER : For myself, without any prophetic vision, and I do not think now it needs any, I believe I can see the the coming result, and its developments may be seen in the progress of our armies, and the necessary consequence which follow them. *I see the masters dispersed, I see the slaves scattered, I see that in all probability they will never be reclaimed no matter what laws we may make. I see the further that progress goes, the more extended will be its effect.*

IN THE HOUSE.

MAY 2, 1862.

Mr. WASHBURNE : But to the battle of Pittsburg Landing. * * *That battle has laid the foundation for finally driving the rebels from the South West.* * History will record it as one of the most glorious victories that has ever illustrated the annals of a great nation.

MAY 26, 1862.

Mr. GURLEY : That the idea of intervention in our affairs has been seriously entertained by the English and French governments, there can be no reasonable doubt. * * Thanks to our sagacious President for dividing the army at the *critical moment,* and ordering all the commanders to advance on the enemy. *This defeated Southern recognition,* for the result was a succession of victories in the West, which saved our Government from so great a humiliation. * * As I have said *the signal success of our arms in the West,* that immediately followed the action of the President *made recognition impossible.*

IN THE SENATE.

JULY 15, 1862.

Mr. HENDERSON : The object of the rebels in the beginning was to build up a confederacy of the cotton States. * * Why did they pretend that they desired the border States to go with them? To make us, in the language of Mr. Yancey, *fortifications* for them; * * to keep armies * * in the border States; * * and by the time their armies were conquered * * our financial condition would be such that we would be *compelled to acknowledge their independence. They hoped that by the destruction of their own cotton, which they thought would regulate matters in Europe, and by keeping our armies at bay in the border States,* * * that could build up a confederacy *commanding the mouth of the Mississippi.* * * *the Gulf of Mexico, the southern Atlantic, and the great rivers of the West.*

Mr. DOOLITTLE : * * We have recovered our rightful supremacy over territories larger than the kingdoms that talk about intervention from Europe—larger than the kingdom of France, three times as large as Great Britain—during which we have *opened the great valley of the Mississippi, that river which more than all things binds this Union together. As long as we hold the Mississippi from its source to its mouth, this Union cannot be dissolved.* New England may regard southeastern Virginia, this side of the Allegany mountains and North and South Carolina, as of very great importance. Why, sir, if we were *ten years* in subjugating that country to the supremacy of the Constitution, it would be as *nothing compared to the holding of the valley of the Mississippi to the Gulf of Mexico, thus binding the Union together from north to south.* * * The history of the world has never shown such a parallel.

JULY 16, 1862.

Mr. CHANDLER : On the 1st day of January, and for months previous to that date, the *armies of the Republic were occupying a purely defensive position upon the whole line from Missouri to the Atlantic* until or about the 27th of January, when the President and Secretary of War issued the order "forward." Then the brave Foote took the initiative, soliciting two thousand men from Halleck to hold Fort Henry after he had captured it with his gunboats.

WHAT PRESIDENT LINCOLN AND MR. SEWARD THOUGHT OF THE CAMPAIGN.

(From the New York Evening Post, February 9, 1862.)

"The President stated yesterday that the recent victory of Fort Henry was of the utmost importance, and was intended to be followed up immediately with a blow on the railway connection fifteen miles from the captured fort, * * that hot work was expected in that region at once, * * *the victories the Government expected to win over the rebels in the next two months would put to flight all thoughts of (England and France) meddling in our affairs.*"

President Lincoln on the 10th of April, 1863, issued the following proclamation :—

"It has pleased Almighty God to vouchsafe signal victories to the land and naval forces engaged in suppressing an internal rebellion, and at the same time to *avert from our country the dangers of foreign intervention and invasion.*"

Mr. SEWARD, March 6, 1863, to Mr. DAYTON, said:

"It is now apparent that we are at the beginning of the end of the attempted revolution. Cities, Districts, and States are coming back under federal authority."

Again, May 7, 1862:

"The proclamation of commerce *which is made*, may be regarded by the *maritime* powers as an *announcement that the Republic has passed the dangers of disunion.*"

APPENDIX 2.

IN THE HOUSE OF REPRESENTATIVS.

FEBRUARY 24, 1862.

Mr. Roscoe Conckling : .I beg leave to offer a resolution, not for action at present, but that it may lie on the table, as follows : " That the thanks of Congress are due and are hereby presented to Generals Halleck and Grant *for planning the recent movements in their respective divisions,* and to both those generals, as well as the officers and soldiers under their command, for achieving the glorious victories in which those movements have resulted."

Mr. Roscoe Conkling : My purpose in offering the resolution, and asking that it may lie over without action now, is this : *I desire that those who earn military honors shall wear them, and wear all that honor to which they are entitled.* I believe the officers named in this resolution are entitled to certain credit, and I desire the resolution to await future action, perhaps amendment, and I care not what particular disposition is made of it for the present. I would like to call up this subject when the House and the country shall be in full possession of all the facts in the case, including reports to be made by different generals, and *when we shall know whether these victories were organized or directed at a distance from the fields where they were won, and if so by whom organized,* or whether they were the conceptions of those who executed them.

Mr. Cox : I should have no objection to this resolution, but I think that it should be a little more extensive. *It seems to be a matter of opinion with gentlemen as to who designed these victories.* I understood the gentlemen from New York the other day, to give a great deal of the credit to the

" Committee on the Conduct of the War." Perhaps the gentlemen will include that in his resolution. One thing is certain, Mr. Speaker, that these resolutions of thanks to our officers ought to be very carefully drawn and very carefully considered *to the end that no one entitled to credit should be excluded from them.* I hope,· therefore, the gentleman will do no injustice to any of those who may be *entitled on further examination to the credit for these victories.*

Mr. ROSCOE CONCKLING : I am very glad the gentleman from Ohio has referred to a remark which fell from me the other day. The remark I made then, and am very glad to repeat now was this, that to that committee, along with other kindred agencies, in which I include the action of the President of the United States and of the present Secretary of War as well as of Congress, were due most vitalizing and important reforms, without which the recent victories might not have been achieved. I will take occasion to say now that I venture to predict the truthful history of these victories will demonstrate that not alone to the mode of doing things, nor to the sources of movements which until recently prevailed in military affairs, not alone to the agencies which were at work when Congress met, not by any means to these alone are to be attributed the brilliant successes in the West. I will hazard the opinion that time will show the value of more recent causes, with a vigorous exercise of power which long lay dormant, itself in harmony with a longing for results and for action, and which has shown itself in debates and proceedings here, and in anxious expression of the people and the press, in every loyal portion of the country. The great necessity of the occasion, the need and the fitness of something more than vague assurances for the future has inaugurated action—resolute onward action—and to this inspirited policy is due movements which have culminated in glorious success. I do not believe the recent movements in the West are a part of any long existing plan conceived elsewhere, and only now unfolding itself. I do not believe these victories were arranged or won by men setting at a distance engaged in what is termed " organizing victory." My belief is, that they have been achieved by bold and resolute men left free to act and to conquer.

* *   Like him, *I should be very unwilling to withhold from a* *single general or officer, be he high or low, a morsel of the credit he deserves,* and my purpose in offering the resolution and asking that it lie over until a future day, is, that *Congress and the country may discriminate and award just praise by awarding it to those who have earned it. I want to crown with heroic honors the real heroes of this war,* and I should be very glad to have the resolution embrace every general and every officer and private who should be included—and my object will be accomplished if the great honor belonging to the blows lately struck on the Western rivers and their banks *shall be conferred where it belongs and shall not be appropriated or absorbed by any person whatever who has not earned it.*

Mr. FENTON: I have drawn very hastily an amendment to the resolution now before the House, which I think embraces the idea which my colleague has just suggested. I offer it, " that the thanks of Congress be tendered to the officers and soldiers who have rushed to arms to sustain the fabric which our fathers erected, and whose devotion has been alike conspicuous, whether in the camp or in the field, whether by that cheerful patriotism and unwearied ardor to be led to the face of the enemies of our country, or their matchless valor in contest."

Mr. ROSCOE CONKLING: I should be |very unwilling to thwart, if I could, any desire my colleague may have, but I submit to him, and I think he will agree with me, that the amendment he proposes is an entire transformation of my resolution and destructive of its object. I mean by the resolution to secure the action of the House, if possible, at the proper time, *in awarding the meed of praise and credit due* to the men entitled, not only to the achievement of these victories, but *for the planning and conception of the movement which led to them.*

Mr. WASHBURN, of Illinois: There is certainly no man here who would withhold his thanks from the two distinguished officers named in that resolution. I feel a peculiar interest in one of them. General Grant, a man I may say here, who is as brave as he is modest and incorruptible. But there are other generals who were upon the field and whom we may wish to thank in the same connection. There is a gentleman who served with us in the last Congress, and in a portion of the present Congress who was upon that battle-field nobly doing his duty, General John A. McClernand.

There is another gentleman a member of the House, I mean Colonel Logan, who distinguished himself gloriously and fell wounded upon that field. And yet there are still other brave officers who were there who should not be forgotten.

Mr. Roscoe Conckling: I took pains in drafting the resolution, though I did it hastily, to so restrict its terms that it could not be at all open to the criticism suggested by the gentleman from Illinois. The resolution declares the thanks of Congress due to those two generals for the movements planned in their respective divisions, not departments, the expression is a departure from strict military phraseology, I believe, and employed to confine the resolution to the *acts* actually done by those named. It was far from my intention to exclude from the thanks to be presented any person who was participant in these movements, and who may properly be included in the resolution.

Mr. Cox: This resolution selects only two of the generals engaged in the recent conflict at Fort Donelson. Generals Halleck and Grant. If, sir, there are any generals entitled to credit for success in that great conflict, General Smith of Pennsylvania, and our recent associate, General McClernand of Illinois, than whom no braver or truer soldier adorns the army of the West, are entitled to an equal degree of the glory, and an equal consideration in the thanks of Congress.

Mr. Holman: I do not want General Wallace to be deprived of his just share of the credit.

Mr. Mallory: Nor should General Buell be forgotten.

Mr. Cox: A splendid list could be made of officers of the army and navy who are entitled to credit for our recent victories. * * The gentleman says he does not believe in organizing victory at a distance. It may turn out when the matter comes to be examined, and fire shall have burned through the smoke, that other generals besides those mentioned—that the General-in-Chief in this city is entitled to some credit, at least for his foresight, design, and strategy, which have so signally contributed to the recent gallant achievements of our army and navy. *It is significant of one directing head and design in these recent victories,* that both flanks of the enemy, west and east, have been stricken and paralyzed at the same time. * * *Let us not, by prejudging this matter, do injustice to any officer of the army and navy.* Let the Committee on Military Affairs have this resolution as they have other resolutions, and let them report a proposition to the House, which will discriminate fairly and justly between the different officers, giving to those who are entitled, not inconsiderately, but with deliberation and care, *the merited thanks of the National Legislature.*

Mr. KELLOGG, of Illinois: I profess to be as justly proud of the victories secured by western generals and western soldiers as any man on this floor, but in our *exultation of great joy over these victories we should be very careful to prevent any injury being done through our action to any portion of the army or to any general engaged in fighting the battles of the Union.* *   * We have soldiers in the ranks fit to be generals. Many such have sacrificed their lives to purchase the victories we have obtained. *   * But, sir, we should not forget to do justice to all—in other words, we should refrain from even indirectly doing injustice to the Commanding General of the American Army.

Mr. OLIN: Those who oppose the resolution offered by my colleague seem entirely to misapprehend the object with which that resolution was offered. *   * *Its objects seems to be to ascertain who it was that planned and directed the military movements which resulted recently in glorious victories in Kentucky and Tennessee.*   *   *   *   *
If it be the object of the House before passing a vote of thanks to ascertain *who was the person who planned and organized these victories* then it would be eminently proper in my opinion to request the Secretary of War to give us that information. That would satisfy the gentleman and the House directly *as to who was the party who planned these military movements.* *   * *It is sufficient for the country, for the present, that somebody has planned* and executed these military movements, *   * still if the gentleman has any desire to know *who originated these movements,* he can ascertain that fact by inquiring at the proper office, for *certainly some one at the War Department must be informed on the subject. The Secretary of War knows whether he had anything to do with them or not—the Commanding General knows whether he had anything to do with them or not*—if neither of them had anything to do with them they will cheerfully say so.

Mr. KELLOGG, of Illinois: In my judgment this resolution, whether so designed or not, is an attack upon the Commanding General of the United States Army. It is declared in express terms by this resolution that the achievements by our arms in the Western Department were the result of movements *planned, organized, and carried out by a subordinate officer of the General Government.* It will be remembered that subordinate officers by law are under the control and command of the Commander-in-Chief of the American army, and that *if there is no general plan, that there ought to be a general plan and system of campaign calculated and designed to put down this rebellion.* I believe there is emanating from the Commander-in-Chief of the American forces, through his first subordinates, and by them to the next, and so continuously down to the soldiers who fight upon the battle-field, a *well-digested, clear, and definite policy of campaign,* that is to be put in motion—*that is in motion to put down this rebellion;* and when a resolution, directly or indirectly, intimates while this should be the case, that it is not the case, and that a subordinate officer has sprung into life and conceived, independently of the military organization of the Government, a campaign and a movement, although resulting gloriously—I say that that is asserted in a declaration, it is a direct charge—I do not say it was intended—that these proper campaigns and necessary movements were not and have not been conceived and put in execution by the Commander-in-Chief of our armies. It is detracting from the General in command of the whole force that which should be meted out to him if in fact he has planned and organized these movements; and I believe here, and I here declare that I believe, that the system of movements that has culminated in glorious victories, and which will soon put down this rebellion, finds root, brain and execution in the Commanding General of the American army and the Chief Executive of the American people, and I would not, by passing this resolution, detract one iota from what he has fairly earned, if this be true, which I believe is true.

Therefore I am opposed to the resolution not from any disrespect to Generals Halleck and Grant, for they have been thanked by the Commander-in-Chief, by the Secretary of War, and more than that by the heartfelt thanks of the American people—a higher tribute than can emanate from any men in position however high that may be.

FEBRUARY 25, 1862.

Mr. THADEUS STEVENS: I rise to a privileged question. I

desire to have entered a motion to reconsider the vote by which the joint resolution tending the thanks of Congress to Generals Halleck and Grant, was referred to the Committee on Military Affairs.

The motion was entered.

MAY 2, 1862.

Mr. WASHBURNE: In time came the operations up the Cumberland and Tennessee rivers, and I state what I know. By a singular coincidence, on the 29th day of January last, without any suggestion from any source, General Grant and Commodore Foote, always acting in entire harmony, applied for permission to move up these rivers, which was granted. The gun boats and land forces moved up to Fort Henry. After that fort was taken it was determined to attack Fort Donelson. The gun boats were to go round and up the Cumberland river, while the army was to move over land from Fort Henry to Fort Donelson.

IN THE SENATE.

MARCH. 13 1862.

THANKS TO CAPTAIN FOOTE.

" Be it resolved,   *   *   *   *   *   that the thanks of Congress and of the American people are due and are hereby tendered to Captain A. H. Foote of the United States navy, and to the officers and men of the Western flotilla under his command, for the great gallantry exhibited by them in the attacks upon Forts Henry and Donelson, for their efficiency in opening the Tennessee, Cumberland, and Mississippi rivers to the pursuits of lawful commerce, and for their unwavering devotion to the cause of the country amidst the greatest difficulties and dangers."

Mr. GRIMES: *A great deal has been said of the origin of the proposition to take possession of the Tennessee river. The credit of originating the idea of a military campaign in that direction has been claimed first for one and then for another military commander.* I desire that impartial justice should be done to every man * * so far as I can learn the project of turning the enemy's flanks by penetrating the Tennessee and Cumberland rivers originated with Commodore Foote. The great rise of water on those rivers was providential, and

with the quick eye of military genius he saw the advantage
it might secure to our arms. Accordingly he sent to General Halleck at St. Louis, the following dispatch:

" CAIRO, *January* 28, 1862.

"General Grant and myself are of opinion that Fort
Henry on the Tennessee river can be carried with four iron-
clad gunboats and troops, and be permanently occupied.
Have we your authority to move for that purpose when
ready?

"A. H. FOOTE."

To this dispatch no reply was vouchsafed, but an order
was subsequently sent to General Grant to proceed up the
Tennessee river, under convoy of the armed flotilla, and attack Fort Henry, directing General Grant to *show* Commodore Foote his orders to this effect.

Commodore Foote was at once ready for the expedition,
and advised the Department to that effect in the following
dispatch:

" PADUCAH, *February* 3, 1862.

"To-day I propose ascending the Tennessee river with
the four new armored boats and the old gunboats, * * in
convoy of the troops under General Grant, *for the purpose of
conjointly attacking and occupying Fort Henry and the railroad
bridge connecting Bowling Green and Columbus.*

"A. H. FOOTE."

After reducing Fort Henry and sweeping the Tennessee
river as far up as Florence, Alabama, Commodore Foote
returned to Cairo to prepare * * for operations against
Donelson. * * He desired a delay of a few days to complete the mortar boats, * * but *General Halleck believed
an immediate attack to be a military necessity.* Although wounded
himself and his gunboats crippled * * he indulged in
no repinings for his personal misfortune. In a letter written
the morning after the battle, to a friend, he said: * * "I
feel sadly at the result of our attack on Fort Donelson. To
see the brave officers and men * * fall by my side
makes me feel sad to lead them to almost certain death."

The next movement of his flotilla was to take Clarksville
on the 19th of February. * * On the 21st of February,
he telegraphed General Cullum, chief of Halleck's staff, as
follows:

"PADUCAH, *February* 21, 1862.

"*General Grant and myself consider this a good time to move on Nashville.* We were about moving for this purpose, when General Grant to my astonishment received a telegram from General Halleck, "not to let the gunboats go higher than Clarksville." No telegram sent to me. The Cumberland is in a good stage of water, and General Grant and I believe we can take Nashville. Please *ask General Halleck if we shall do it.*"

A. H. FOOTE."

It may be that there was some *great military reason* why General Grant was directed "not to let the gunboats go higher than Clarksville," but up to this time, it is wholly unappreciable by the public.

The next fact of importance in the campaign at the West, and indeed the most important of all was the evacuation of Columbus. *Why was this strong hold* which costs so much labor and expense *abandoned without firing a shot?* It is well understood that *Commodore Foote was opposed to giving the rebels an opportunity to leave Columbus.* He felt sure of his ability with his gun and mortar boats to shell them into a speedy surrender, but was compelled to give way to counsels of military commanders. * * The *two arms of the public service are equally entitled to the credit of frightening the rebels from their strongest position on the Mississippi river, if not the strongest in their whole military jurisdiction.*

N. B.—At the time Congress was considering the question—*who originated the idea of a military campaign on the line of the Tennessee river* there were present on the floor a few Senators and Representatives who were aware that Miss Carroll, as early as the last of November, 1861, devised and recommended to the Government the adoption of *that line of attack upon the Confederacy—they* having seen and read her *plan*, but, who, from prudential considerations, gave no publicity to their information.

ERRATTA.

Page 2, 8th line from top, read *then* for "their."
Page 11, 23d line from top, read *on* for "in."
Page 18, 21st line from top, read *change* for "exchange."